Catalina

The Adlers

By
Avery Gale

The Adlers

The siblings. Their occupations and ages at the beginning of the series:

Austin – 31 – CEO of the family oil conglomerate based in Austin, TX. Married to magical, Charlotte.

Asia – 30 – Ruthless legal eagle for the family business. Married to Franklin Cordesi.

Bronx – 29 – Owns a string of car dealerships in partnership with brother, Cleveland. Married to Kenya Star.

Cleveland – 28 – Race car driver. Astral traveler. Married to Vienna Quan.

Brooklyn – 27 – Retrieval expert for big insurance companies. Semi-retired in subsequent books. Security consultant. Married to Luke Grayson, lives in New Mexico. Daughter, Crystal.

Catalina – 26 – Freelance intelligent agent working with the CIA, MI6, Mossad, and others. Travels the world as a successful jewelry designer.

Israel – 25 – Security expert and tracker. Married to shifter, Dr. Bristol Banks.

Kensington – 24 – Actor. Married to Denali West.

London – 23 – Chemist/Researcher. Married to shifters, Elijah & Evan Monroe. They live outside Boston and have twin sons.

Paris – 22 – Recent College Graduate. Mated with Sheriff Trinity Stone. School Administrator and teacher.

Cooper once told her, "You are a work of art, Catalina. The Renaissance Masters would have revered you. Wordsworth, Keats, and Shelley would have immortalized you with their most romantic sonnets." The words were forever written on her heart, their impact so much greater than he could ever imagine.

Prologue

C ATALINA'S KNEES TREMBLED, knocking together so violently, she hoped they wouldn't fold out from under her as Cooper drew lazy circles around her throbbing clit. How he thought she would be able to narrate the magical ceremony taking place in front of them was a mystery for the ages. There were standing in the shadows, but she was sure they were still visible to anyone making a minimal effort to search them out.

Damn, the man knew exactly how she responded to his touch, and she was enough of an adrenaline junkie to feed off the energy created when there was a risk of being caught. Cooper Hicks could turn her inside out with frustration, then switch it all up and light her up with little more than a whispered word. His touch intensified until it sent her spiraling over the edge as the light show from the ceremony lit up the sky, and a split second later, Lilly West's damned bazooka shot from a boat anchored in the lake. An orgasm, so powerful she dropped into his arms, was the third element in the trifecta of erotic moments.

"Your trust is my most treasured possession, Princess." Cooper's whispered words wafted over the shell of her ear, sending a shiver up her spine. He was a man of many talents... seduction ranking dangerously close to the top of the list. "Let's get this debrief done. I've missed you, and I intend to fuck you until we both lose our damned minds."

There was something he wasn't telling her. Catalina was a lot of things, but she wasn't naïve. She'd worked with Cooper enough to know it was pointless to ask. Cooper Hicks could not be coerced into surrendering information until he was ready. For tonight, she would try to set it aside. She was anxious to wrap up the debriefing and get back to Adler Oil.

Catalina was the first to admit the past few months had been physically and emotionally draining. Walking barefoot over hot coals with the devil nipping at her heels would have been a walk in the park compared to being kidnapped and held hostage. Reliving the terror of those interminable days left her unable to sleep and presented an enormous roadblock to her healing.

If it hadn't been for the man currently leading her up the grassy slope to her brother's house, Catalina knew she would have died in the filthy cell where she'd been confined. Hell, the only time she'd stepped outside its confines was when her captors tortured her. After she was released from the hospital, Cooper stayed with her in a hotel until her injuries healed enough, her family wouldn't go batshit crazy when they saw her at Austin and Charlotte's wedding. Their reaction to her emaciated state had been bad enough.

Moving from New York back to Texas to set up her own storefront on the ground floor of Adler Oil's downtown building proved to be her saving grace. Throwing herself into work until she was running on fumes was the only way she could sleep longer than a few hours. Thankfully, her business wasn't up and running when a political faction she'd never heard of decided she was public enemy number one. Shuddering as a flashback assailed her, Cat stumbled, the world around spinning faster and faster. Before she could take another step, Cooper's arm tightened around her waist.

When had he let go of her hand and secured her to his side? Before they stepped into the light flooding the bustling patio area, Cooper pulled her to the side of the walkway and into his arms. With a quick turn, they were facing one another without a breath separating them.

"How often does this happen?" Catalina considered opting for denial, but pretending she didn't know what Cooper was talking about would be impossible to pull off. He knew her too well. He must have sensed her hesitance because he gave her shoulders a squeeze to emphasize the fact she hadn't answered. "Stop trying to figure out a way to lie, Princess. You and I both know it won't work. I know all your little tricks, and I'd much prefer the rest of the night be about pleasure without any reason to punish you for lying."

Yeah, Cat wanted to cast her vote for cutting straight to the mind-blowing pleasure part of this evening's activities as well. Skirting around a conversation she'd rather avoid was preferable to confessing she was slowly drowning in flashbacks and nightmares. The line between memories and premonitions was starting to blur... and that was the heart of the problem. She knew once she started this conversation, he wasn't going to let it go. *Fucking hell.*

"I'm coping... the dreams started right after you left."

Cat wasn't ready to admit she didn't have nightmares when he held her during the night.

"There's more. Tell me." Cooper's tone was implacable. She'd pushed him far enough.

"I understand the flashbacks and nightmares. Hell, as much as it humbles me, I'm not going to deny the truth—when you hold me at night, it chases the fear away." He didn't interrupt her, but when he caressed the side of her face with the pads of his fingers, Cat couldn't hold back her soft moan. Leaning into his touch, she pulled in a deep breath.

The moment she met Cooper Hicks, Catalina knew they were fated mates. It pissed her off at first because his arrogance grated on her last nerve. Due to her frustration, the first few years, their relationship drifted from adversarial to professionally distant. After a night of drunken sexual abandon at the end of a successful mission in Indonesia, Catalina learned two things. First, she had a submissive streak a mile wide when it came to Cooper. Second, no other man would ever earn her trust—he was the only man she would ever let dominate her.

"Lately, there have been dreams that don't reflect what has already happened. They feel more like premonitions... and they are terrifying." He tilted his head to the side ever so slightly, studying her. She sensed he was trying to assess how far to push at the moment. Goddess above, she had no idea how to mention elderly witches and black slime—he'd lock her in the nearest padded room and throw away the key. Before he could ask any of the dozens of questions she was certain were floating around in his sharp mind, she blundered ahead.

"Can we get the debriefing over and then get to the wild monkey sex? We can talk about the gloom and doom stuff later. Unless you've changed your mind, and in that case, I'll catch a ride back to Prairie Winds with the Wests."

What am I supposed to do when the man who drives me insane also drives me wild, fulfilling my every sexual fantasy? Poke the bear with a long stick, then run before he eats me alive.

Chapter One

C ATALINA FELT THE shift in Cooper the moment the taunting words passed her lips. The man might not be a shifter, but he was a predator all the same.

"You're too smart to throw out such a ridiculous challenge, Catalina. Tell me what you're afraid of—and I want to remind you, omitting pertinent information is still lying." She'd been so focused on the way his hands slipped through the folds of her dress to grip the cheeks of her ass in warning, she almost missed the question buried skillfully in his censure.

Cooper was one of those rare examples of a recruit surpassing the skills of his mentor. He'd soaked up everything Cameron Barnes taught him like a sponge, then added his own experiences and observations to the mix. Cooper was nearly impossible to fool when she was fully on her game, and tonight, Catalina's libido wasn't letting her function anywhere near her peak.

Refocusing on their conversation, Cat realized whether they were dreams or premonitions didn't matter as much as the toll they were taking on her. He'd seen through her attempt to goad him, and his response was a testament to his training as a Dominant The most aggravating part was his utter mastery of self-control. She watched the steady rise and fall of his chest as his pulse throbbed steadily beneath the surface. Her wolf scented nothing but concern. He wasn't angry or frustrated—those two emotions changed a person's body chemistry much the same as fear, the scent easy for a shifter to detect.

Damn, damn, fuck it all. He was right, she was deflecting. Ordinarily, Catalina approached everything head-on, but as unnerving as it was to admit, she was afraid. Afraid to admit her growing concern for what was coming, afraid she wasn't going to be able to shield her family from the dark side of magic still lurking in the background, and most of all, afraid she was going to end up heartbroken when it was all said and done.

"All of it, Princess, spit it out. Remember, I can't hear what you're thinking, although I'd probably be able to make a couple of reasonable guesses." He tightened his hold on her ass cheeks. His grip wasn't painful, but the message was clear—he wasn't going to back down. "The foundation is always trust, Catalina. Your safety is my number one priority, but I need your help. I'm playing from a disadvantage since I don't have your magical abilities. I need your help when we're dealing with forces I don't fully understand."

Nodding her understanding, Catalina took a deep breath, trying to steady her nerves. With her family nearby, there was a real possibility one of them would pick up enough of this conversation to start asking questions. Cooper was the only one who knew the details of her captivity. If it hadn't been for his tenacity, she'd have died in that small cell without anyone ever knowing what happened to her. Everyone she loved would have been forever haunted by the fact she'd simply vanished. Cam Barnes had been instrumental in smoothing the continuing issues of diplomatic fall-out, but it had been Cooper who'd stormed in with guns blazing to pull her out of hell on earth.

Briefly outlining the dreams she'd been having wasn't as difficult as she'd thought it would be. Cooper wasn't pressing her for details, but Catalina knew the hard questions had to be asked... eventually. The simple truth was, she had a lot more questions than answers.

"I want to sit in on the debriefing. Hell, it'll be worth our time to find out where the hell Lilly got her hot little socialite hands on that kind of firepower." Cat couldn't hold back her smile. Lilly West was a firecracker of the first order. Her love of powerful guns and explosions was only eclipsed by her loyalty to the people she cared about. Kent and Kyle West owned the Prairie Winds Club and managed several freelance special operations teams. Their wife was a handful, and their kids challenged their parents at every opportunity, but it was Kent and Kyle's mother, Lilly, who challenged them at every turn.

"If I were you, I'd be reluctant to ask about the gun. Consider it a... well... sort of a don't ask, don't tell situation. It's probably best to maintain some level of plausible deniability with the Agency." Catalina leaned into him, grinning, grateful for the break in the tension between them. Walking into the light, Cat found herself pulled into so many hugs she lost count, but it was Charlotte standing to the side holding baby Marshall who caught Aunt Catalina's attention. Making her way quickly to stand in front of her sister-in-law, Cat held out her arms and noted the relief in Charlotte's expression.

"Thank you. My arms were starting to go numb. Why does everyone assume new mothers don't want to share their babies? It's a big heap of donkey dung. I speak for new moms everywhere when I tell you—we're exhausted. Take the baby... bring him back next Thursday. I just want to take a nap." Cat tried not to snicker but knew she hadn't fooled Charlotte. "Go ahead and laugh, but someday, you'll find out I'm right. I have two nannies, and I'm still up to my ass in alligators. I kept up with your demanding brother and his obsessive-compulsive fraction-of-a-minute calendar without batting an eye, but one tiny human is draining me... literally."

Charlotte's maniacal laughter was a little frightening, and their conversation was beginning to draw unwanted attention. Austin's wife wasn't usually given to dramatics, but with her arms windmilling and her non-stop chatter, the performance was edging close to Oscar-worthy.

"You think I'm kidding about the draining thing? Nope. Absolutely a fact. *Nursing is good for the baby. You have to do it for the baby. The baby doesn't get all the important antibodies if you don't breastfeed.* There isn't a woman on the planet who isn't given a ticket for this guilt trip... that sucker's a one-way coupon, too, let me tell ya. Then they give you a machine that works way too much like the milking machines I saw once at a dairy farm. It's just wrong... and hysterically funny on so many levels." Catalina stared at Charlotte as huge tears filled her eyes. The petite beauty started to sag just as Austin and Bristol appeared at her side.

"Come on, little mama, let's get you inside. I think I can help." Dr. Bristol Adler, Israel's new wife, was Charlotte's obstetrician and personal physician. Bristol was one of the most sought-after specialists in the state for good reason. No one was surprised by the exponential growth of Bristol's private clinic; the woman was as compassionate as she was brilliant. Dr. B had also made it her personal mission to cater to magicals and kinksters. According to Israel, his mate nearly worked herself to death before she'd been able to recruit a quality physician to join her growing practice.

Austin scooped his wife into his arms, and Catalina's heart ached for Charlotte. Her sister-in-law was going to be mortified when she was feeling more like herself and realized how public her melt-down had been.

We won't let her be embarrassed. That's what family does, Cat.

Israel's smooth voice moved through her mind, making her seek him out. He was standing a few feet to her left, and when their gazes met, he made a point of looking at the sleeping infant in her arms.

What's your plan for our nephew?

Holy fucking hell. What was she going to do with a baby? She didn't know anything about babies. Well, she knew they leaked, and you had to feed them a lot... which was probably why they leaked so much. She'd visited her sisters after they'd had their children, but she hadn't been actively involved in caring for their children. Feeling herself start to panic, Cat was shocked when Cooper stepped in front of her and took the baby into his arms.

"Come here, little man. Your aunt looks like she is closing in on a panic attack. How about you hang out with me until Tobi or Lilly realize I've got you." Catalina stood with her mouth open, staring in disbelief at the man she thought she knew so well. When Cooper finally looked up at her, he looked bewildered.

"What?"

"I had no idea you knew anything about babies. How did I not know this?" Catalina wasn't going to deny she was impressed. "People don't surprise me very often, but you have shocked me to my toes." She almost laughed out loud at the irony. Cat had been on missions with Cooper when the situation was so hot, neither of them knew if they'd get out of it alive. During her rescue, she'd watched him kill more men than she wanted to count—the path he cleared to pull her out of hell had been wide and bloody.

"I'm trying to decide if I should be pleased, knowing I was able to surprise you or insulted you didn't think I spent time with my niece and nephew." How could she have forgotten his younger sister and her husbands had children? Not only was she an incompetent aunt, apparently, she wasn't a particularly good friend, either. Looking at her, his gaze softened before he continued.

"I love how Lakyn's men have no interest in knowing who the genetic father of either child is, even though it's easy to figure out. Little Cooper is three and already taller than most five-year-olds. Leiloni is all dark eyes, soft ebony curls, and beautiful bronze skin that makes her look like she just returned from a Caribbean cruise."

Listening to Cooper wax poetic about his niece and nephew made her realize how little time she'd spent with her own. She popped in when she could, showered them with gifts, took their mamas for spa days, then disappeared for months at a time. She'd held the babies for photos, then quickly handed them back to whoever was closest. The contrast between them was damned humbling as she watched Cooper Hicks, former US Navy SEAL, CIA operative, and sexual Dominant, handled baby Marshall like he was born to the job. The whole evening was edging dangerously close to bizarre.

A few minutes ago, Cat hadn't been able to think about anything beyond several rounds of swinging from the chandeliers, wild monkey sex. How in the hell had she gone from raging hormones to watching Cooper rescue her nephew from *her*? She was getting damned tired of all these humbling moments. Catalina had been snatched off the street in Bum-Fuck-Nowhere before she had even checked in to her hotel. The torture and beatings she endured came damn close to breaking her spirit. Two things kept her from giving up—hearing her mother pleading for her to hold on just a few more hours and her certainty Cooper was doing everything in his power to find her.

"You shouldn't have blocked me, Cat." Israel surprised her by speaking at her side rather than into her mind. She tried to smile but didn't think he was fooled when his brows drew together. "Don't even try it blow smoke up my ass, sister." When he turned to face her, Cat mirrored the action, facing the brother she shared a special bond with because he could read her so easily. "I appreciate your effort to protect me, hoping I wouldn't go out of my mind with worry, but blocking me was worse. Feeling your panic, followed by nothing but deafening silence was terrifying." He pulled her into his arms, hugging her so tight, Cat heard herself squeak. "Don't do it again."

The surge of emotion washing over her made it impossible to speak around the lump in her throat. The backs of her eyes burned, and she dreaded the tears she knew would follow. Crying sucked. Some women looked sweet and vulnerable when they shed tears—Cat looked like she'd gone a few rounds in the ring with... hell, what was his name? The guy with the strange face tattoo who did cameos in movies. Geez, what was wrong with her? Giving herself a mental facepalm at her lack of sports knowledge, Cat couldn't hold back her laughter when Israel laughed and provided Mike Tyson's name through their shared link.

"It's interesting you used a boxing reference when you've always given me and Austin hell for following the sport." Giving her a final squeeze, Israel released her but only put a few inches between them. She watched as he gave someone behind her a quick nod before his attention once again centered on her. "When you are ready to talk, I'll be here."

"Thank you. I'm not sure when that will be, but I'm working on it." She wasn't working on it intentionally, but she had little choice. For the moment, all she could do was try to cope with what was being thrown her way.

"Hand him over, Cooper. You get plenty of baby time with Lakyn's angels." Lilly West's voice filled the area around them. She'd swooped in on Cooper, lifting Marshall from his arms. Cat didn't know anyone who didn't love the gorgeous West matriarch. Lilly was an inspiration in so many ways. Stunningly beautiful, a familiar face in too many social circles to count, and a wild card.

"If you're going to baby-snatch, you have to tell me about the gun. Holy hell, there isn't enough left of those guys to get a positive ID." Cooper grinned at Lilly, but her gaze never left the sleeping infant cradled in her arms.

"Did you see Grandma Lilly toast those two water intruders, Marshall? The bad guys were going to hurt your family, and that wasn't acceptable, so I brought out the serious artillery. I'm already teaching my grands how to shoot, but that's a secret, so don't tell their anal-retentive dads. You'll learn soon enough—sometimes it is best to play your cards close to your chest."

"We know you are teaching the kids to shoot. If you thought the range owner wouldn't call us, you've forgotten he's a member of the club." Cat wasn't surprised to see Kyle West step out of the shadows. He might be retired from the Special Forces, but he was still a trained operator. The man could write a book on stealth movement and had an uncanny ability to be in the right place at the right time.

"I don't have a problem with you teaching them the basics, but we're drawing the line at explosives. Your granddaughter is too much like you for anyone's comfort." Kent's comment drew Lilly's attention away from Marshall.

"That's the nicest thing you've ever said to me. I'm thrilled you think she is like me and overjoyed to know it gives you pause. It has never been my intention to make you or your brother comfortable. Challenging you has always been my greatest joy." Her saccharin tone belied her words, and anyone with a Southern mama would recognize the slap down Lilly had given her sons.

Del and Dean West, Lilly's husbands, both coughed,

trying to cover up their laughter, even though no one else standing in the small circle made any attempt to hide their amusement. The woman was the absolute embodiment of Southern belle—sugar sprinkled with lots of spice.

Chapter Two

A N HOUR LATER, Cooper and Catalina finally escaped the debriefing from hell. If anything could derail a room full of trained operatives, it was exposing them to the world of magic. For the first half-hour, members of the Prairie Winds team were solely focused on the things they couldn't explain. One thing Cooper had learned about military hotshots, they could—and would—analyze shit to death, but in the end, they always integrated any new intel and never looked back.

As they approached his truck, Catalina reached for the door handle—again. The swat Cooper gave her was sharp enough to lift his lovely mate off her feet.

"Princess, I've warned you more than once. Unless we are running for our lives and those few seconds separate life from death, you wait for me to open your damned door."

Cooper knew she was distracted and had simply forgotten. She'd given him the perfect opportunity to use the lapse to bring her focus back to the moment, and he'd taken it. He planned to fully explore whatever challenges she was facing, but he needed to get her home first. He knew Catalina Adler better than she knew herself—she was the most open when she was sexually sated. The endorphin high was as close to truth serum for the stunning shifter as anything he'd found, and he planned to ensure they both enjoyed the process.

"Yes, Sir." Her response was perfect, or it would have been if he didn't suspect it was edging dangerously close to contrived. Catalina was only submissive to him even then, they were continually engaged in a power struggle. Cooper had never met a sub who could top from the bottom more subtly than his Princess. If they gave out trophies for finesse, she'd have dozens lining the shelves of her suite at Adler Oil. Lifting her into the truck, Cooper stroked his fingers along the underside of her chin before fastening her seat belt.

"As much as I'd like to take you to the club and let every Dom there give you two swats, I want you draped over my knees more. I'm looking forward to watching the creamy skin of your ass cheeks bloom the first shades of baby pink. Seeing the soft shade of my handprint darken to vibrant rose before the intensity of the strokes darkens the marks to glowing a heated scarlet is hedonism at its finest. We're both going to enjoy it—I promise. And to be perfectly honest, I'm not in the mood to share my visual pleasure." The challenge Cooper saw flashing in Cat's eyes was one he wouldn't allow to go unmet.

"I'm going to push you, Princess. Are you up to it? Perhaps you've forgotten how much freedom you have found in submission? I promised to take you to places you'd never imagined possible." Cooper paused, watching her as a predator studies its prey.

One of the things she'd always struggled with as an

operative was patience. She tended to give up on stakeouts too soon, rushing in where angels fear to tread, as his mom used to say. When Cooper was on a mission, he was the epitome of patience. There were times she'd asked him if he was human. Cooper smiled to himself, remembering the few times Catalina had tried to outfox him and discovered it was impossible. One of Cooper's greatest strengths was thinking several steps ahead. She'd asked him about it once, and he'd likened it to playing three-dimensional chess, the best analogy he could give her.

"THE ONLY WAY you are going to rest properly is if you put yourself in my hands again, Princess. I have fulfilled my promise every time you have gifted me with your trust. Give yourself to me tonight, Catalina. Tell me you want what only I can give you."

He was right… on all counts… *damn it.*

She'd dated other men in the intervening years after their first scene. Cat stopped accepting those invitations when it became clear no other man compared to the one standing beside her. Cooper was both her greatest annoyance and greatest fascination, wrapped in every physical trait she found attractive. The man was the very definition of hot. Cat had seen women walk into walls and street signs because they were distracted, looking at him. When she drew it to his attention, he'd simply laughed it off.

Sighing to herself as they prepared to drive back to Austin, Catalina realized Cooper knew more about her kidnapping and injuries than anyone else. Her sister-in-law,

Charlotte, learned more than Catalina was comfortable with when the magical healer hugged her. Charlotte healed Cat instantly, taking on the physical injuries Cat tried to conceal before quickly healing herself. Austin's bride had also gotten a brief glimpse at the horrors Cat endured. Charlotte steadfastly refused to share the information with anyone else in the family, and Catalina was eternally grateful the gifted healer kept her confidence. Austin had been both frustrated with his new wife and impressed with her integrity.

"You have to say the words, Cat." Once again, Cooper's fingers slid slowly down her cheek, leaving a trail of blazing heat in their wake. They weren't formally mated, so she was shocked to her toes to hear his voice float through her mind.

I want to collar you, baby. Damn, I wish you would agree to be mine.

"Please, I need you." Four simple words choked around the lump in her throat, but they were enough. Cooper closed the door, stalked around the truck, and they were on their way before Cat could sort out the deeper meaning of what she'd said. Catalina had always known she was a conduit for the other side but was still shocked to hear her mother speaking so clearly, she turned to see if Cooper could hear her as well.

Darling, girl, why are you afraid to admit Cooper holds your heart? Your magic will unlock his, and Cooper's love will amplify yours. Be brave, my sweet risk-taker. History isn't made by those who live in fear.

COOPER DOUBTED CATALINA knew how much she'd revealed when she admitted her need for him. The darned woman's line between annoyance and anticipation was microscopically narrow, and Cooper was the only one who could ride the razor's edge with any measure of success. When he'd learned she tried dating after he'd introduced her to Dominance and submission, Cooper had remained patient. His prediction had been spot on—*damn it.* She'd never seen the same man more than twice and hadn't slept with any of them.

Stepping back had driven him crazy, but he'd known she needed time to come to terms with what happened between them. He was convinced once her sexual identity had been challenged and expanded, it would never be the same. Biding his time tested his patience on too many levels to count. They'd worked with each other several times recently, their rapport growing as the snark settled to a manageable level. Cooper suspected the sass would return in spades the first time he tried to rein her in. *Bring it, Princess!*

His phone vibrated in his pocket, signaling an incoming message. Cooper grimaced when he saw the text was from Cameron Barnes. Cam was many things—kink club owner, Dom, husband, father, loyal friend. The man was one of the best operatives the Agency ever produced, and for that reason, the powers that be were reluctant to let him go, so retirement remained elusive. Random was the one thing Cam was not—if he was contacting Cooper, there was a reason.

I saw you leave, and if I'm reading your body language right, your sub is in for a long night. Start in the garage. I've instructed the Adler Oil building's security team to cut the feeds from your parking area to the entrance of Catalina's suite. You have thirty minutes from the time you punch in your code to open the gate.

Cooper smiled to himself. Cam's ability to be in the right place at the right time was uncanny and handy as hell in this case.

"Should I be worried about that message?" Cat tried to modulate her tone to sound casual, but he knew her too well to fall for the ruse. She was curious and more possessive than she would ever admit. It didn't matter that she was facing the other way, Catalina was as well trained as any operative he'd ever worked with. Her environmental and situational awareness was so good he'd often assumed she was using magic.

"Probably." He let the word linger for several long seconds before continuing. "It seems I'm not the only Dom who thinks you've earned a punishment." He didn't hear a sharp intake of breath, and she hadn't moved a muscle, so Cooper had no idea what she was thinking.

"Cam always has his nose in everyone's business." When he flicked a glance in her direction, Cat shook her head and chuckled. "He was standing among the ornamental pampas grass near the back corner of the house." This time he heard the fatigue and resignation in her tone. "I'm a shifter, Cooper. It's humbling to realize you know me so well in many ways but continually forget about one of the most significant aspects of... well, what makes me, me."

Son of a fucking bitch, she's right. She hadn't made the

comment to knock his arrogant ass off his high horse, but damn if she hadn't dished up a healthy serving of humble pie.

"You are right, Princess. There are so many beautiful layers to your personality. I could peel back one, only to reveal another every day for a millennium and never learn all your secrets." Her shoulders relaxed, and he saw rather than heard her sigh. She'd told him once she often felt like an outsider in her own family—the comment shocked him at the time, but after spending a considerable amount of time with the Adlers, he'd seen how it was possible.

After Catalina's confession about feeling disconnected, Cooper made a concerted effort to call his little sister more frequently and truly listen to what she had to say. Six months ago, the two of them had been enjoying a glass of wine and watching the stars twinkle in the moonless Texas sky, and Lakyn asked him what prompted the change. She confided what a huge difference it made in her life and subsequently, their relationship. When he'd explained what happened, Lakyn advised him to use the lesson wisely, applying it to the relationship he was building with Catalina. *My sister is wise beyond her years.*

"Tomorrow morning, you and I are going to eat breakfast on your deck." Cooper smiled to himself when Cat's brows drew together in confusion.

"Isn't it supposed to rain all day tomorrow?" She was trying to bait him. The little minx knew exactly how far she could push him.

"It is, but it's also supposed to be unusually warm, so it won't stop us from enjoying the small, covered space. We have things to discuss, and I don't want to run the risk of someone interrupting us." He'd considered using the rooftop terrace, but it was a popular retreat and used by too many members of the Adler family to ensure their privacy.

Asia Adler had talked her brother into relinquishing a large portion of the top floor, and she'd used an equal share of the second floor. Combined, the square footage created a two-story outdoor living area, unlike any other Cooper had ever seen. The entire family used it as their own, but he needed a much more intimate space for the discussion he had planned. It was time to begin pushing his feisty sub, keeping her off base until her head recognized what her heart already knew—they belonged together. Since they were getting close to Austin, where they'd be driving under regularly spaced streetlights, it was time to challenge her.

"Lift your skirt out from under you, Princess. I want your bare ass on the leather seat." He heard the hitch in her breathing and could already predict what her protest was going to be, so he decided to head it off. "Your wet pussy is not going to stain the leather." When she reluctantly complied, he gave her an approving nod. "Good girl. Now, pull the dress to your waist and spread your knees as far apart as you can." This time she didn't hesitate as long, and he rewarded her with a sexy grin.

"I can smell your arousal, Catalina. Knowing you are slick, your body readying itself for my possession is fucking hot." The earthy scent of her pussy intensified to the point, Cooper was having trouble focusing on anything else. "Lean your seat back a little, Princess." He heard the small electric motor beneath the passenger seat whine for several seconds and smiled when she automatically tilted her hips, giving him the view he wanted. "Jesus, Joseph, and sweet Mother Mary, you are a fucking goddess."

Cooper knew Cat had designed an extensive line of jewelry for Doms who wanted to decorate their sub's *pink bits*—her words, not his. Personally, Cooper didn't find the word cunt offensive. Hell, it was a reasonable term to use when describing where an exquisitely crafted piece of jewelry would be located. He could still remember the fire flashing in her eyes as she informed him the word wasn't acceptable for marketing for too many reasons to list.

Cooper helped himself to several pieces from her inventory before they left for the magical ceremony at her brother's lakeside home. Cooper suspected the sparkling jeweled clips, which didn't require piercing, were going to sell faster than she could produce them. Cat would need to hire a battalion of artisans or become more automated at some point in the very near future.

Cat didn't have a playroom in her suite yet, but over the past couple of days, Cooper had managed to add a few concealed enhancements to her bed, and he was looking forward to revealing them. Once she was bound for his pleasure, he'd spread the lips of her labia wide and use the pieces he would pay her handsomely for. When all her secrets were exposed to his view, he would bring out the new toy he'd bought for her before her kidnapping. The small, low-voltage ultraviolet light would provide the perfect edge to send her soaring.

Reaching over, Cooper trailed the tips of his fingers over the smooth skin of her mound before letting them slide into the wet folds. Goosebumps raced over her skin, but she didn't move.

"Perfect. I love how responsive you are, Princess. Seeing you struggle to stay still when I know how much you crave a firmer touch pleases me more than you know." Removing his wet fingers from her pussy, Cooper brought them to his mouth to suck them clean. "You taste so sweet. I'm anxious to get the first part of our scene over with, so I can enjoy lapping the sweet cream coating those smooth pussy lips."

Keying in his personal code to open the gate of the secured underground parking garage, Cooper bit back a smile when he saw her muscles tighten. He knew she was worried about the security cameras—a reasonable concern since she didn't know the feeds were down for the next half hour. Pulling his truck into one of the parking stalls reserved for the Adler family, Cooper gave Cat a pointed look, making certain she remembered to stay put until he opened her door. Watching her through the windshield, he saw her pull in a deep, shuddering breath. Catalina might think she was bracing herself for what was to come, but he knew she was already spinning out of control.

He didn't bother holding out his hand and letting her step down from the truck on her own, slipping one arm behind her bareback and the other beneath her knees. Lifting her from the truck, Cooper sent up a silent prayer of thanks the dress he'd bought her was a halter. Feeling the warmth of her bare back and legs cradled in his arms ramped up his desire when he wouldn't have thought it possible. Once he'd set her on her feet, it only took one quick move for the front of her dress to drift down to her waist. She instinctively moved to pull the flimsy garment back into place, but his sharp command to stop froze her in place.

"You have put yourself in my hands before, Princess, and it opened up a whole new world for you." The spark of fire in her eyes assured him the observation was dead-on. "Hell, you've put your life in my hands on numerous occasions. I'm asking you to trust me once again. Trust me to know what you need. Trust me to keep you safe and to never put you in harm's way—either physically or emotionally." He hoped the repeated phrase would drive home her need to put herself in his hands without reservation. Trust was the key.

Physically, Catalina was fully recovered, and from what he'd seen, stronger than ever. Emotionally, Cat was still fragile. In many ways, Cooper worried she was edging close to shattering, and he hoped tonight would give her the outlet to release some of the turmoil battering her from the inside. Damn, brilliant women always amazed him. They were usually too strong for their own good.

It was damned frustrating to know Catalina still blamed herself for her kidnapping, claiming she should have been more aware of her surroundings. Logical arguments weren't getting him anywhere. Cam Barnes was equally frustrated with Catalina's insistence that everything was fine when it was clearly not. Watching her now, uncertainty reflecting in her gaze, Cooper resisted the urge to pull her into his arms and assure her everything was going to be fine. He refused to patronize her with platitudes he had no way of knowing were true. He could assure her he was in it for the long haul, but he doubted she was ready to hear it.

No, now wasn't the time for a heart-to-heart chat—

they would both be better served if he'd follow through on his original plan. Catalina must have sensed the shift in the direction of his thinking and known he'd refocused his attention on her. Letting his eyes track over her in a slow slide, he smiled when her nipples peaked so tight against the flimsy fabric of her dress, they probably ached.

"Hand me the dress, Princess. I'm going to save it since it's become one of my favorites." He watched her, wondering which force was going to win the battle he saw raging in her eyes. Would she trust him or let her insecurity and fear trump his command? Cooper let out a breath he didn't know he was holding when she let the dress fall, grabbing it easily before it hit the concrete floor. Cat handed the delicate piece of clothing to him, and he saw the effort it took for her to release her grip on the fabric. "Thank you, Princess. Your trust is a gift I treasure."

Catalina kept her eyes on him. He knew she was struggling not to scan the area around them. As a trained operative, it would be difficult for her not to succumb to the need to assess any potential for danger. Keeping her focus on him was a huge compliment, one he made a mental note to comment on later.

"Turn around and spread your feet slightly more than shoulder-width apart, then bend at the waist and grasp your ankles." He'd planned to give her a few swats before they entered the elevator but decided to reward her compliance with a little teasing instead. Once she was in position, he smoothed his hands over the globes of her ass, doing his best to ignore the fading pink scars. Every time he saw the remaining evidence of the time she'd spent in the clutches of evil, his gut churned. "You have a spectacular ass, baby." He grinned when she gasped. Since he rarely called her anything other than Princess or her name, he knew the endearment was unexpected. "Toned muscles under the creamiest skin in the entire world. Perfectly rounded handfuls just right for grasping when I'm fucking you."

Stepping to the side so his leg braced her shoulder, Cooper gave her two sharp swats before slipping two fingers into her vagina, pressing against her G-spot. Cooper wasn't surprised when the walls of her sheath pulsed around his fingers. She'd been strung tight all evening, and he'd done his best to keep her on edge. When he felt her tipping closer to release, Cooper pulled his fingers free and helped her stand. Weaving as the blood that had pooled in her head drained quickly back south, she looked dazed for several seconds. He understood the feeling. His brain was frequently drained of oxygen-rich blood as it filled his cock anytime he thought about her. Holding her upper arms until she was steady on her feet, Cooper pressed his lips to hers in a gentle kiss meant to settle rather than inflame.

It was time to move If he didn't get her upstairs in the next fifteen minutes, the security system would be back up. He didn't want Israel Adler's team seeing more of the boss's sister than they should. Once inside the elevator, he turned her to the wall, placing her hands against the wall.

"Spread your legs and arch your back." The position lifted her ass into the perfect position for the heated swats he intended to give her Once she was in place, he let the doors slide silently closed and pressed the button for her floor. The small car was so quiet, he could hear the small hitches in her breathing as she tried to anticipate what he planned to do. When he saw her eyes flicker to the security camera in the corner, he knew it was time to proceed.

"One for each floor, Princess." Her look of confusion dissipated quickly as he made certain the slaps were spread evenly over her pert ass. By the time the elevator car passed the third floor, Catalina was lifting into his swats, her soft moans filling the luxurious space as the smell of her arousal replaced the scent of polished wood and freshly shampooed carpet.

The Adler Oil building was one of the wonders of the universe, in Cooper's opinion. The damned place was always pristine, but no one ever saw the cleaning crew. He had no idea how they managed to do so much and remain virtually invisible, but it was damned impressive.

The sound of his palm meeting her bare flesh was music to his ears. Increasing the intensity of the swats made her moan, and he had to fight the urge to plunge his fingers as deep as they'd go in her tight sheath. *Fucking hell, this has to be the slowest elevator on the planet.* Cooper could have sworn he heard Israel laugh and shook his head to clear the strange sensation. *I don't know if I'll ever get used to hearing people speak into my mind.*

When the elevators soft ding signaled their arrival, Cooper breathed a sigh of relief. If he didn't free himself from the confines of his jeans soon, his damned dick was going to have a permanent zipper tattoo. Wrapping his large hand around her small wrist, Cooper led her out of the elevator before turning her to face him.

"Are you wet, Princess?" She didn't waste any time confirming what he already knew. "I want you to turn around and walk slowly to your door while I play with you. Don't stop, no matter what I do. Keep moving, Princess, or you'll find sitting awfully painful for the next several days."

"Yes, Sir." Catalina's tone was wary, but she'd spoken without any hesitation, so he gave her a quick nod. Before she could take the first step, Cooper pushed his fingers against the crack of her ass then slide the tips of his calloused fingers between her legs.

"You're soaked, Catalina. Knowing you are so responsive is fucking hot." Having his fingers buried in her sex forced Cat to walk much slower than she ordinarily did. Cooper sensed her desperation to get into her suite before losing control of her release, but he wasn't in the mood to be accommodating.

Rotating his fingers until they pressed against the spongy spot at the front of her channel, Cooper felt her body respond a split second before she stumbled. He'd been prepared and caught her easily. Using his free hand, he encircled her upper arm, careful not to bruise the underside of her bicep. They stepped over the threshold into her suite, and he smiled when she visibly relaxed.

"Did you think I would let anyone look at what I consider mine, Princess? I would have thought you'd know me better. I'm looking forward to our scenes at the club, but allowing other like-minded people to enjoy the view is entirely different." She spun around so fast, his fingers slipped from the warmth of her body before he could still her movement. The fire in her eyes left no doubt how pissed she was, but he wasn't going to apologize for her erroneous assumption.

Chapter Three

C ATALINA OPENED HER mouth to read Cooper the riot act, but he pressed a finger against her lips and shook his head. "Think before you speak, Princess. Are the words you are about to utter going to get you what you want... will they move you closer to the satisfaction your body is screaming for?" He watched as she took a shuddering breath, trying to rein in her frustration and anger.

Although Cooper hadn't lied to her, he was certainly guilty of deceiving her by omission—something he was sure she would point out in the future. Hell, if she was anything like his sister, she'd throw it in his face anytime it suited her. Cooper fought the urge to smile, thinking about all the spankings she would be getting in the future when she argued the point. He knew what it cost her to remain silent, and he rewarded her with a quick kiss.

"Wise choice, Princess." His quick kiss to the tip of Cat's nose seemed to surprise her, making him smile when her eyes widened at the unexpected gesture. "Darlin', I have been looking forward to this for longer than I care to think about. It's been too long since our last scene, and I think we both need this."

Cat was strung tight and had been for months. Several

31

members of her family had messaged him, expressing concern she was headed for an emotional crash, and he agreed. Catalina's coping method of choice? Work. Cooper planned to show her there were other options, which might not be as lucrative, but they were damned well more fun.

CATALINA FOUGHT THE urge to tell Cooper to either get on with it, or she'd dig one of the BOBs out of her nightstand and take care of things herself. Thinking about how he would react made it damned difficult to keep a straight face. The spanking he'd given her in the garage and elevator wound her up so tight, she'd been a hot second away from spontaneous combustion before he stopped, leaving her struggling to regain her bearings.

Walking the short distance from the elevator to her door with Cooper's fingers wreaking havoc in her core tested her concentration in a way nothing ever had. The man was lethal in so many ways, Catalina was beginning to think the great Goddess and Fate were toying with her. Maybe he wasn't her mate but was put in her life to be the fire that tempered her steel. Doing a mental facepalm at her own wishful thinking, she refocused her attention on the man watching her with avid interest. Catalina wondered what Cooper had planned—his expression gave nothing away. Whatever he had in mind, she hoped it involved enough orgasms, she'd collapse from sheer exhaustion.

Doctors at the military hospital stressed the importance

of following up with a counselor once she returned home, but Catalina knew the Agency she'd been working for wouldn't appreciate her divulging the juicy details of her mission. Chatting up a perfect stranger without security clearance would paint a target on her back... a bigger one than she suspected was already there.

The man who'd ordered her kidnapping claimed she was carrying a list of suspected double agents. His intel was flawed, but not as much as everyone believed. Catalina received the list several days earlier than planned, and knowing how sensitive the information was, she'd destroyed the small slip of paper after committing the names to memory. When she was debriefed at the military hospital, Catalina gave the Agency she'd been working for everything she could remember. The interrogators suspected there were more names than she'd reported, but she'd hit a wall. The harder she tried to remember, the more agitated and frustrated she became.

One of the United States Diplomatic officials who'd insisted on sitting in on the interview suggested hypnosis, but she'd refused. One of the hazards of freelancing was protecting a myriad of secrets. Allowing an agent from one of the alphabet agencies she worked for the opportunity to poke around in her head was a mistake she wouldn't make.

Cooper and Cam were the only people in Austin who knew how precarious the situation was, or so she'd thought until tonight. The knowing looks she'd gotten from Kent and Kyle West spoke volumes. Just the thought of the danger she might bring to her beloved hometown made her head spin.

A streak of fire blazed across both ass cheeks, pulling

her back to the moment. Blinking several times, trying to clear the cobwebs from her muddled thinking, Cat wondered what the hell that awful shrieking noise was filling the air around her. Was that incessant keening coming from her? Fucking Freddie Fox and a hotrod, she couldn't lose it now. Cooper already thought she was dancing on the outer rim of the sanity bell. She'd never get a damned orgasm if he believed she was some kind of emotional invalid.

Suck it up, Cat, you can do this. She could. She would. Fuck, why wasn't her self-talk working? It was supposed to help. All the frick-fracking self-help books said positive self-encouragement could hold back the overwhelming waves of panic many PTSD victims experienced. *Damn it all to hell, why are there black dots dancing in front of me, and what the fuck... are they getting bigger?*

"Catalina." Cooper's voice sounded like a whip cracking beside her. Cat involuntarily recoiled before the warmth of his bare chest pressed against her, the soft hair teasing her nipples and providing a welcome distraction. When had he taken off his shirt? How long had she been traipsing around on her little mental field trip?

"It breaks my heart when you flinch away from my touch. My only regret about your rescue is not getting the chance to kill the bastards twice." She knew he would have liked to torture her captors. He'd told her he would have loved the opportunity to make certain they understood how it felt to be brutalized before he sent them screaming into the depths of hell. Cat hoped the bastards' souls ran into a brick wall of karma the next time they decided to incarnate.

After a few late-night drinks on the rooftop terrace, she and Asia decided it took four lifetimes of penance to make up for one life behaving like an asshat. Her sister hadn't asked questions, and Cat appreciated her unconditional support. The night had been therapeutic on too many levels to mention. Catalina had been secretly celebrating Cam's earlier call, letting her know Cooper was on his way home. Asia had been happy to join her, but from what little her older sister had said, she was in seriously hot water and not looking forward to answering to her husband, who stood silently in the shadows, watching over them.

Franklin Cordesi assured Catalina he was only there to provide an additional layer of security, but she suspected he was there to make certain his lovely wife didn't try to make a break for it. Asia was a force of nature in both the courtroom and the boardroom. Corporate rivals called her the Adler Ice Princess for good reason. The Adler siblings liked Franklin, even though his introduction into the family had been questionable. Having been hired to seduce Asia's sister, London, he'd found himself treating her like the younger sister he'd never had. In the end, he'd saved her life and set the stage for her to share her medical discoveries with the world.

"I SWEAR TO all things holy, I wish I could hear what you're thinking." Cooper shook his head as he held Catalina in his arms. Since returning to Austin, he'd started to hear bits and pieces but could never make out enough for all the pieces to fall into place. He'd spent several hours talking to

Audric Stafford, surprised by how in-the-know the head of the Magic Council was about the world of espionage. Hell, the man's intel concerning the countries Uncle Sam was worried about was better than the CIA's, but the most valuable information had been much more personal. Audric's only words of caution had been about protecting the beautiful woman pressing herself like a second skin against his chest.

"Catalina possesses magical gifts far more powerful than she knows. The Council of Magic has been monitoring her since she was a toddler, knowing the gifts would manifest suddenly. She is what we refer to as *The Keeper of the Promises*. The future of the magical world manifests itself every generation, and Catalina's future will be filled with revelations. We wanted her to be prepared for their strength and the changes they would bring to her life. In the interest of transparency, you should know, her entire career as an agent was part of her training." When Cooper started to argue, Audric shook his head.

"I didn't say it was handed to her. Your agency recruited her for a reason—don't ever underestimate the connection between the world of magic and government entities. They may not officially recognize us, but they are more than happy to utilize our power anytime they deem it useful."

Cooper waited for Audric to continue, frustrated when the wizard's phone distracted him. Before he walked away, Stafford leaned close and whispered, "Her kidnapping and rescue set things in motion. You'll feel the shift in her energy. As your connection grows, so will your ability to hear her. Listen closely."

The advice rolled through his mind as a surge of energy warmed him from the inside out. Cooper might not ever fully understand the way magic worked, but he damned well recognized the way it felt.

"It seems I'm not the only one who's easily distracted." Catalina's voice was tinged with amusement and impatience, the latter giving him the perfect excuse to give her ass another heated caress.

"Point taken, Princess. My momentary lapse of attention is going to work in your favor this time." He'd told her once how much he loved watching the way her pupils dilated when he deepened the timbre of his voice, explaining how her responsiveness kicked his need for her into high gear. Catalina had been surprised by his candor. Cooper's entire adult life had centered on secrecy, making his openness even more significant.

She wasn't sure what he had in mind but hoped like hell it involved the release her body was craving. The fire he stoked in her core was burning hot, despite what she knew was an outward appearance of calm. Years of working covert ops trained her to blank her expression, but her body's response to this man was the equivalent of shouting her need from the rooftops.

Watching in disbelief as Cooper leaned down, hefting her over his shoulder, Cat squealed as he started walking down the short hall to the master bedroom. She jerked upward when he pushed a finger through her wet folds—evidently, the damned digit had a homing device—sliding in effortlessly.

"Watch your head, Cat. We wouldn't want you to get a concussion."

Oh yeah, she could only imagine how fun that would be to explain to the local emergency medical services. Austin was, for intents and purposes, a small town. The Adlers were well known, and an ambulance call to Adler Oil at this time of night would no doubt garner a lot of attention. *Yeah, hard pass on that golden opportunity, thank you very much.*

Cat's breath caught when Cooper released her legs enough to allow her body to slide sensuously down his own. Before her feet were solidly on the floor, his voice rumbled from deep in his chest.

"All the way to your knees, Princess."

She'd given him blow jobs several times, but something told her this time was going to be different. Settling on the pillow he dropped to the floor, Cat leaned back on her heels as Cooper pulled his belt from his waist and set it aside in plain sight. Everything the man did was calculated, and she knew this was no exception. The belt was a reminder of how quickly the entire scene could shift to something much more painful.

It took all her control to keep from shoving Cooper's fingers aside so she could open his fly and pull his cock free. The outline of his erection was clearly defined by the soft, well-worn denim of the jeans he wore. The evidence of his arousal made her mouth water. Unconsciously licking her lips in anticipation, Cat didn't try to hide her need.

"You look hungry, Princess. I have just the thing for you." Pulling himself free, Cat watched as he stroked his length several times before threading his fingers through the long tresses of her hair. "The last time I saw you, your hair was flame red Catalina. I like this much better. Rich chestnut, streaks of honey, and sunlight framing your face… it suits you perfectly." When she tried to lean forward to lick the pearly drop of pre-cum at his tip, Cooper shook his head.

"We'll go at my pace. Your pleasure belongs to me, Catalina. Your orgasms are mine to give or withhold." He studied her, waiting for a reaction, but she knew he wouldn't see anything but heated desire. She nodded her understanding, although she hadn't been focused on his words. Hell, the way her gaze was locked on his cock should have probably made him uneasy. "Show me how much you want my cock, Catalina."

PUSHING HIMSELF CLOSER, Cooper groaned out loud at the sight of the creamy white pearl at his tip, painting her kiss-swollen lips. Wrapping one hand around his base, she slipped the tip of her tongue into his slit, burrowing as far as possible in her effort to gather the last remnants of his natural lubricant, setting his entire body aflame. Before he could comment, she opened her mouth and sucked him all the way to the back of her throat. Cooper locked his knees and prayed he wouldn't embarrass himself by coming faster than an Olympic downhill racer.

Catalina's soft laughter moved through his mind, letting him know she'd been listening in on his thoughts. "I'm going to talk to your lovely sisters-in-law about blocking. Until then, I'll monitor my thoughts anytime I'm not keeping you properly occupied. I think an extra-large vibrating butt plug might keep you from eavesdropping.

What do you think, Princess?"

He doubted she would take his threat seriously, but she should. His club bag was well stocked and sitting on the floor of her walk-in closet. If he had his way, it wouldn't be long before they had the entire floor to themselves. The remodeling project he was planning included a playroom to rival those of the best kink clubs in the world. He'd already secured the other apartments and cleared his plans with Austin.

Before her kidnapping, Catalina was actively involved in every aspect of the remodeling plans, but everything was put on hold while she recovered. After returning to Austin, he'd ramped up the schedule while Cat focused on her new business. Cooper hoped his mental review of the architect's drawings would be enough distraction to keep him from succumbing to the temptation of her mouth. Lightning streaked up his spine, setting fire to a short fuse—*yeah, that plan didn't work for shit.*

"Fucking hell, your mouth is devil-blessed, sweetheart." The fingers he threaded through her hair tightened enough, she gasped around him. "It's too good, Princess." Pulling back, he shook his head at the annoyed look he watched flash in her eyes before it was masked. She loved pushing him past his limit, seizing power from him, topping from the bottom, but this was a power struggle he didn't plan to lose. As difficult as it had been, Cooper found the strength to pull from her mouth, immediately missing the feel of her tongue bathing the underside of his cock.

"Up you go." He didn't wait for her to stand, preferring to lift her himself. "Get up on the bed, face down, ass up. Let your feet fall over the edge." When she was in position, he slid her knees farther apart and gave her exposed pussy lips a quick slap. "Don't move, sub. Your body is mine to enjoy, and I have a lot planned." Taking two steps back, Cooper watched as cream eased from her vagina, coating the tender folds.

"I have a design project for you, my sweet sub. I want a pretty bauble that will keep these pretty pink folds open, something that will let me sit in the chair behind me and admire the view. Watching your pussy cream from my words alone will be one of my greatest pleasures." Using the tip of his finger, Cooper traced a line along the sensitive crease at the top of her thigh. "Gold-plated titanium chain so you don't break it when I do this." Slapping the flat of his hand against her pussy, the blow sounded much harsher than it was, but her reaction was perfect.

"See? You couldn't hold still." Reaching beneath the mattress, Cooper pulled out the restraints he'd put into place before they left for Bronx's lake house. Wrapping the straps around her thighs, he pulled the thick strips of nylon tight before securing the Velcro ends. "Much better. The view from here is spectacular." Leaning down, Cooper pursed his lips and blew cool air over her exposed sex. This time, she shuddered but was unable to move her legs in spite of her desperate grasping the bed covering beneath her.

"More. Please. I need you to touch me, Cooper... Sir."

"Valiant effort to save yourself, Princess, but it seems to have fallen a bit short." Another slap to her bare cunt, this one sharper than the first, drew a cry from her lips. Cooper knew he hadn't caused her any significant pain, but he certainly got her attention.

"I'm sorry, Sir. I wasn't trying to be disrespectful. I'm desperate… and falling over the edge of control. There is a storm brewing, and I'm not sure I can stop the surge that's coming. I need to release some of the power before it levels me."

Cooper was stunned. The words were laced with a level of anguish far beyond sexual submission. He'd gotten the raw honesty he was seeking without pushing as hard as he'd feared he would be forced to. Slapping her bare folds again, he pushed two fingers through the flexing muscles of her opening until the calloused pads of his fingers pressed against her G-spot.

Hearing Catalina screaming his name as she shattered was the hottest thing in the world. Damn, he was going to have to be careful, or she was going to own him body and soul. Laughing at his own foolishness, Cooper wondered when he'd started lying to himself. The woman had owned him since the first moment they met. The smell of her release was sweet and made his cock so hard, he was afraid it would split apart.

Moving around the bed, he positioned himself in front of her and waited. When she came back to herself, he helped her up onto her elbows before pressing against her lips.

"Take me, Princess, make me come and swallow it all." He noted an odd crackling sound surrounding them, reminding him of the powerful static electricity domes he loved as a kid. Watching the brightly colored lightning flicker beneath the glass as it followed his fingers had always fascinated him.

Cooper wasn't sure how he knew something had

changed, but the shift in Cat's energy was undeniable. She sucked him into her throat and swallowed around him, the sensation so intense, he felt his head fall back as seed burst from his tip. The pulses so strong, each one bordered on painful. Brilliant bursts of color rained down behind his eyelids, and he found himself gasping for breath. Heat surged through his body as a flash of white-hot pain seared the inside of his thigh.

For several seconds, Cooper was sure his mind was imploding before the world around him slowly came back into blurry focus. His brain felt like it had exploded as black dots floated in front of his eyes, and his body felt so odd, he had no words to describe it. He'd never had an orgasm like this one—the release defied description. Finally regaining his senses, Cooper looked down to see guilt in Catalina's eyes as she pressed the flat of her tongue against two small punctures on the inside of his thigh. Holy shit, she'd bitten him—they were mated.

Cooper hated seeing the remorse in her expression. Damn, she had to know this was something he not only expected but wanted. Fucking awesome was the first thought that came to mind, and he swore some of the tension drained from her back and shoulders. Everything he'd learned about shifters over the past several years reinforced the connection he felt to Catalina. This was a step in the right direction, but only one of several he hoped they'd share in the near future. He needed to clear this up right now.

Chapter Four

CATALINA WAS LOSING her damned mind. What had she been thinking? Mating with Cooper without talking to him first had been a reckless and selfish move. Yes, they'd talked about it in generalities, but she'd gotten carried away when his scent ignited a soul-deep instinct she hadn't known existed until it crashed over her.

The man had studied shifters like it was his damned job, and at this point, he might well know more about her kind than she did. The moment her elongated canines pierced his skin, she'd felt their souls meld together. His words drifted through her mind as soon as his eyes opened, and their gazes met. Hearing his reassurances, their mating was something he'd wanted, eased her guilt.

When he pulled back, putting space between them, she felt the loss of his warmth and shivered. As a shifter, Catalina was rarely cold, but this was an entirely different kind of chill—this was the absence of a touch she craved like a drug. Cooper Hicks was her personal brand of heroin, addictive as hell and the basis of more bad decisions than she wanted to think about. As he walked around behind her, Catalina started to worry about what he planned to do.

"Stop worrying, Princess. I'll undo the restraints before your muscles seize from being in the same awkward position for too long. We'll take a nice long bath and talk. I have questions, and now that your thoughts are open to me, our conversations will be much more interesting."

Oh, yippee, there's news worth celebrating... not!

He disappeared down the hall, giving her instructions to start the bath and use plenty of bubbles. She laughed when he returned with the two glasses filled to the brim and a bottle tucked under his arm.

"Planning to drink it all, are we?" Hopefully, a bit of teasing would ease some of the tension she was feeling.

"Shifters metabolize alcohol much faster than nonmagicals, or so I'm told. I think we should test the theory." His unrepentant grin made him look much younger than she knew he was. The laugh lines at the corners of his eyes made her wish they were deeper. The man was so damned handsome, he made her eyes hurt, but sadly, he didn't smile nearly enough.

In the years she'd known him, Catalina had watched him walk through everything from sleazy bars to high-end eateries catering to the rich and tanned, and the reaction was always the same. Men and women stopped speaking mid-sentence to stare, waiters walked into walls, and dancers fell off stages as their attention was pulled in his direction. The most amazing part was how oblivious he seemed to the attention.

Settling down in the steaming water, Catalina moaned as her muscles started to relax. Hell, she hadn't realized how tight her thigh muscles were until she stretched them out. Cooper handed her one of the glasses, grinning when she drained it. Refilling her glass before climbing in behind her, she saw him drain most of his own drink before pulling her against him until her back rested against his chest.

"Before you dig yourself into a pit of worry and despair, I want to tell you how pleased I am with what happened a few minutes ago." Cooper's words were spoken quietly against the shell of her ear, the warmth of his breath as reassuring as what he'd said. She knew her brothers had struggled with the same issue, but being in good company didn't justify her actions. "Let it go, Catalina." Cooper's voice was sharper this time, the commanding tone putting her on alert—he wasn't going to tolerate her feeling guilt when he'd gotten exactly what he wanted.

"I should have given you a choice. There isn't any excuse for my lack of self-control, but I don't regret it either—does that make any sense?"

"Princess, I've wanted you as my own since the first time I saw you." She felt his chest vibrate as he chuckled and cupped her breasts in his large hands. The pads of his index fingers found their way to her nipples, the calloused pads of his fingertips tracing around the areolas sending heat surging through her system. "That isn't to say I haven't wanted to throttle you a time or two—but something tells me that sentiment is one you've shared more often than not."

Cooper was right. The first year they'd known one another, they'd butted heads on everything. It was her sister, Asia, who'd pointed out their bickering was little more than a type of foreplay. At the time, Catalina scoffed at the claim, but her denial had fallen on deaf ears. One of Asia's many remarkable gifts was her uncanny ability to read people. As the second oldest, Asia had often been a surrogate mother to her younger brothers and sisters, and the experience taught her to cut to the chase like a damned surgeon.

"Asia was right. It was foreplay, even though we might not have recognized it right away. Truthfully, I thought you were annoying me deliberately. Cam was the one who assured me that wasn't the case. As disbelieving as you were with Asia's spot-on assessment, it pales in comparison to how pissed I was when Cam called me an arrogant putz." Catalina couldn't hold back her laughter. She had no trouble believing Cameron Barnes had said exactly that. "Cam and Asia are cut from the same cloth—their view of the world centers around the theory it was best to run to the roar." Before she could argue the point, Cooper continued.

"Cam was the one who told me what that expression meant. I'd heard people use it but hadn't understood the significance. Hearing his explanation about the way lions tricked their prey into running to the strongest and most aggressive among them fit perfectly into so many of our operations. Putting the oldest lion on one side, his fierce roar frighting prey, sending them running opposite direction was a great analogy for covert operations. So often, the success or failure of our missions hinged on an agent's ability to distract their mark."

"I know I can't go back." Cat wasn't sure why she'd spoken the words out loud. Hell, she'd barely admitted them to herself. There wasn't an agency in the world that would hire her now. Everything about her last job had gone from sunshine to shit so quickly, the assignment probably set some kind of land speed record. It didn't matter how small or insignificant the job, there was no room for an agent who many considered unstable. The intelligence community wasn't as large as most people believed, and people talked. Cripes, in Cat's opinion, the male agents she had worked with were among the biggest gossips in the world. There wasn't a chance in hell they didn't all know what happened to her and how she was still struggling to pull the last names from the depths of her memory.

"No, you can't. You've been compromised, but if I'm not mistaken, you wanted out anyway."

Cooper was right. She'd been ready to walk away before she'd agreed to the last job because the money had been too good to pass up. Her instincts had shouted at her how important it was to get her hands on that list. Pain lanced through her head, making her groan as she held her breath, trying to stay as still as possible until it passed. Cooper's arms encircled her, the heat of his body so much more intense now that their DNA was coursing through one another's veins.

"I did, but no one wants to leave with a cloud hanging over their head." Cat wasn't naïve. She knew people would question whether or not she was faking. Hell, if the circumstances were different, she'd be wondering the same thing about a fellow agent. Many of them had to be asking who she was protecting. Another stab of pain beneath her forehead made her drop the empty wine glass, and it shattered on the tile floor, the tinkling sound of breaking glass making her curse.

"Watch your language, Princess. You are too smart to fill your mouth with filth." He'd warned her about her language before, paddling her ass when she'd forgotten and rehearsed every foul word she knew. She'd likely get another spanking for her latest outburst once they cleaned up the mess she'd made. Right now, she'd welcome the distraction.

COOPER NEEDED TO get Catalina's mind off the damned list. The longer this fiasco continued, the more convinced Cooper was he knew who she was protecting. He needed to talk to Cam, but first, he had a mate to care for. Stepping carefully from the tub, Cooper swept the glass aside with a towel before lifting Catalina from the water, not setting her down until she was safely inside her walk-in closet.

"Find a robe and sturdy shoes. We'll clean up the glass before we chat about your language." He almost laughed out loud at the look on her face. If he didn't know how much she enjoyed being draped over his lap, her beautiful ass peaked perfectly for his hand, Cooper might have fallen for the stricken expression. It only took them a few minutes to clear the bathroom of broken glass. Cooper shook his head slowly when Catalina would have walked past where he sat in the living room.

"Come here, Princess. We have something to discuss." Standing in front of him, she shifted one foot to the other, fidgeting nervously. He enjoyed watching her squirm but also suspected she was a hot second away from flipping from nervous anticipation to deliberate defiance—the second wouldn't get either of them what they wanted. "Over my lap, Catalina. Last time, I gave you ten for your foul language. Since that doesn't appear to have been sufficient, we'll double that number tonight." When her eyes widened and she started to speak, he shook his head.

"Do you trust me, Catalina?" It wasn't as simple a question as it first appeared. Her subconscious was struggling, but he hoped she would mitigate her immediate response enough to let her confidence return to the surface. In the end, he wanted to distract her enough that the memories she was trying to suppress would have a chance to return.

"Yes. I've trusted you with my life just as you have trusted me with yours." Cat's answer was perfect and spoken without any hesitation. He had no idea how much he valued her trust. Once she was in position, he didn't give her time to fall into fear. The swats dropped quickly, and he made certain to spread them out over both cheeks, with emphasis on the tender crease at the top of her thighs. Sitting would be uncomfortable for several days, and he hoped the reminder was more effective this time.

Cooper realized his hearing was sharper and his sense of smell more acute as her gasps caught his attention and the scent of her arousal surrounded him. By the time he finished, Catalina's entire body was shaking in anticipation. Slipping his fingers into the gap at the top of her thighs, he was pleased to feel her slick cream. Hell, she was so wet, his jeans were already damp, and more honey clung to the inside of her thighs.

"Ask for what you want, Princess."

"Please, Sir, I need to come." Whispered between shallow breaths, it wasn't eloquent, but it was enough.

"Who do you belong to, Catalina?"

"You. Only you." Her words set his soul on fire, and all he could think about was fucking her with his fingers until she screamed his name as her honey coated his fingers. Her entire body arched before deflating over his knees. Pulling his fingers from her after he milked the final spasms from her sex, Cooper took several seconds to appreciate the view before rolling her over to cradle her in his arms.

Knowing he and Catalina would be staying in Cam and CeCe's small guest house during the renovations, he'd worried she wouldn't be comfortable outside the small bubble of Adler Oil. Hearing her declaration of trust put his mind at ease. The small structure, which was attached to the family's palatial lakefront home, had a separate entrance and a safe room. Cam offered to let them use the space after their beloved nanny moved into one of the lower-level Adler Oil suites.

Lindy Timish recently passed the bar exam and accepted a position with one of the most prestigious law firms in Austin. Having worked for the Wests and Barnes, as well as Austin and Charlotte Adler, Lindy had acquired four powerful and wildly overprotective guardians. Cooper had shaken his head as he'd listened to the strategic planning session the four men held at the Wests' office a few weeks ago. You'd have thought they were plotting the takeover of the free world.

Three weeks earlier

COOPER AND ISRAEL stood together, leaning against the back wall of the spacious office, watching in dismay.

"If they think they're fooling Lindy, they are the most naïve bastards to ever grace the damned planet." Israel's observation was as amusing as it was accurate. As gifted as Israel Adler was, Cooper knew he'd likely been listening in on the young woman's thoughts. Israel's quick nod confirmed Cooper's suspicion. "Lindy knows the Fearsome Four plan to railroad her into choosing an apartment that meets their ridiculous criteria for approval."

"Why do I think Lindy's being coached by CeCe, Tobi, and Charlotte?" Cooper knew all three women were fond of the younger woman who'd helped them raise their children. When Cam and Dr. Cecelia Barnes' children no longer needed a nanny Lindy had seamlessly transitioned to household manager and occasionally worked for the Wests. Most recently, she pinch-hit as a nanny for Austin and Charlotte until theirs arrived. She'd helped train the new caregiver, making certain Marshall had the best possible care.

"Don't forget Asia She's had her fingers so deep in this pie, her elbows are sticky sweet. Franklin warned her to stay out of it. I'm sure you can imagine how that went over." Cooper wanted to laugh at Israel's observation about his sister.

"Franklin seems more than capable of managing his lovely bride." Cooper's respect for Franklin Cordesi had grown by leaps and bounds since they met several years earlier. People didn't surprise Cooper very often, but

Cordesi hadn't been the criminal everyone assumed he was. "I assume Cordesi has been doing what he does best, working quietly behind the scenes.

"It's a given. If you ask me, Audric is mentoring Franklin. Austin mentioned there are well-sourced rumors floating around that my new brother-in-law has already taken a seat on the Magic Council." Israel's information matched what Cooper heard earlier from Cam, but it still surprised him the man had flown so far under all their radars. The energy in the room shifted, pulling Israel and Cooper's attention back to the meeting.

Kyle West leaned back in his well-worn leather wingback office chair, studying his friend and neighbor. Ordinarily, Kyle wasn't an easy man to read, but the expression he leveled in Cam Barnes' direction was crystal clear. None of them had ever seen Cam flustered, but it was easy to see he was slipping damned close to the end of his rope. Before Cooper could step forward, Israel's hand wrapped firmly around his forearm as he gave an almost imperceptible shake of his head.

"Cut to the chase, Cam. We all know you and Cooper are the names Catalina has blocked out. Why don't you level with Lindy? Tell her the real reason she needs to take the apartment at Adler Oil." Fuck, Cooper should have known the Wests were too well connected to fool. Unfortunately, the more people who knew, the more difficult it was going to be to protect Catalina from the memories haunting her.

"I can't prove it, and Cooper hasn't been able to find any corroborating evidence, but that's our best guess. At this point, I don't think it matters if she remembers or not.

Lindy is connected to us—all of us—in too many ways. I want her to be safe. She's important." Cam's shoulders sagged as if he'd been carrying the weight of the world.

"Ladies, let's move this to the kitchen where we have wine. This conversation is about to go off-rails." Tobi led the women out, closing the door behind them. Silence filled the room, and Cooper frowned. Of course, it mattered if Catalina confirmed their names were on that damned double agent list. If anything happened to him or to Cam, Cat would be forced to live with the guilt once the memories came flooding back—and Cooper didn't doubt for a moment they would return in an avalanche of emotion.

"I agree it would be nice to have confirmation, but I'm not convinced it's critical to our mission, which is keeping the three of you alive." Turning to Cooper, Kyle asked, "Does Cat know you are home?"

Fuck, straight to the heart of it.

"Not yet. She didn't need to be here for this meeting. I know she is looking for me, and she's been closing in fast. I wish she would take some time and recover. Hell, I'd prefer she stay inside the damned Adler Oil building, but I don't believe that's a reasonable expectation." The other men around the room chuckled, knowing full well, Cat wasn't bound by logic. Cooper stepped closer to Kyle's desk—it was time to get everything out on the table. "We don't know for sure how many names were on the list she was given. If there are other names, we need to know what their connection is to Cat."

A silver thread of smoke appeared out of nowhere, circling until the spiral suddenly vanished, revealing Audric

Stafford seated in a chair in front of Kyle's desk—an ornate chair that hadn't been there a few seconds earlier. Cooper had to give the man credit—he knew how to make an entrance.

"Personally, I think you have... what is that expression about fish you Americans are so very fond of?" Audric was dressed in a morning coat, crisply pressed matching pants, tie, and spats.

Fucking hell, spats? Really? Where in the hell had the man been before his dramatic arrival?

"It was theatrical, wasn't it? In my position, I don't get to have much fun, but I'm thoroughly enjoying Texas. The people here live large—it's refreshing. Coming here gives me a chance to enjoy a bit of flair. Now about that saying..."

"Bigger fish to fry?" Lilly West sauntered into the room as if she had every right to be there, her husbands grinning when they stepped in the door behind her. Kyle groaned, but his brother had the good sense to temper his reaction. "I heard that, Kyle." Lilly cast her son a dark look. From the chagrined look on Kyle's face, it didn't matter how old a man was—his mother's glare still had the power to make him cringe.

Audric stood, giving Lilly an appreciative nod, and winked before returning to his seat. Kent chuckled when his fathers both rolled their eyes. The elderly wizard was a shameless... and unrepentant flirt.

"Audric, care to enlighten us? I'm sure I speak for the entire team when I tell you I'm wondering about those bigger fish." Kent was the more tactful of the two West brothers, but contrary to what most people believed, he was as impatient as his twin. Cooper had heard members of Kent's former SEAL team refer to him as silent but deadly. He was one of those operators who sat back, watching and waiting in silence, ready to strike at precisely the right moment. Kent appeared more affable, but it was a ruse, a fact Audric Stafford would not miss.

"We have people on the inside, and they are convinced the Agency was testing Catalina. The entire mission was a sham." Cooper felt every muscle in his body tense in response. For a few seconds, a red haze blurred his vision, a clear indicator his blood pressure had just jumped off the chart. He'd never had a problem controlling his anger until Catalina—she was his weakness, his Achilles heel.

During the first couple of years they worked together, Cooper did everything in his power to keep away from Catalina, knowing it would be impossible to hide his attraction to her. Something at her very core called to him in a way he couldn't understand. It wasn't until he learned more about her kind and the soul-centered pull of mates, it began to make sense.

"I think you are a man of many talents, Audric—master magician, skilled negotiator, devoted father, and grandfather. All of those are valuable traits, but what I believe you are missing is a chance to remember how it feels to be young and in love. Everyone in this room saw Cooper's reaction to your comment about Catalina. Painting someone into a corner during a rare moment of emotional vulnerability is beneath you, Mr. Stafford."

Cooper was stunned. He'd heard Southern women could cut you off at the knees without out blinking, burying you so deep in sugar it became quicksand. This was the first time he'd seen this side of Lilly West, and his heart squeezed, knowing she'd taken up for him against the most powerful and politically connected wizard in the world.

"Well-made point, Mrs. West." The man turned to Cooper, his expression filled with remorse. "I'm sorry, Cooper, you didn't deserve that. I don't know why I tossed you under the... rail... no, subway... drat."

"Threw you under the bus. Father, we're going to have a long chat about your obsession with American slang." Brigitte Stafford walked into the center of the room, sparkles of light floating from the hem of her flowing dress. Turning to Cooper, she shook her head. "What are you doing here? Fucking fudge-covered frogs, I just finished redirecting Catalina... again. She's going to strangle her contact for sending her from one continent to another, looking for you. She thinks you're in danger, and here you are, sitting in Kent and Kyle's throne room, watching their sweet mama tear off a piece of my father's hide." Soft laughter filled the room, and Lilly's cheeks blushed a delicious shade of baby pink.

"Catalina is so desperate to find you, she isn't being careful. Her carelessness is much too dangerous." The room erupted into action, every voice offering a solution. The noise was deafening before a loud whoosh of air brought blessed silence. It took Cooper several seconds to realize he was sliding feet first through a clear tube surrounded by the most vivid swirls of color he'd ever seen.

The movement of the swirling color was disorienting, but the longer it lasted, the more accustomed he became to the sensation. He'd felt the hair on his arms standing on end a fraction of a second before being surrounded by light. The shift in the energy surrounding him was unmistakable, easily recognized after spending time with magicals. There weren't a lot of common elements among the magicals he'd met, but their ability to channel the power surrounding them was always present. There were times Cooper was damned envious of their magical abilities, despite recognizing the crushing responsibility that accompanied the skills.

With a resounding thud, Cooper found himself standing in front of the hotel where he'd been staying before Audric whisked him back to Texas. Now that he thought about it, he was getting damned tired of being launched around the globe like one of the pneumatic bullets banks used for their drive-in facilities. *I feel like I've just been turned into one of those freebie mini suckers the bank tellers send to kids after you make a deposit—Audric deposited me in Texas, and Gigi sent the sucker back to BFE.*

Chapter Five

CATALINA GASPED WHEN the first swat landed. Damn it, this was the second time in as many days she'd been spanked, and this time, Cooper wasn't playing. She wasn't sure why he was being such a hardass about her language, but she had noticed most of the Doms she knew shared his aversion.

"You need to stay in the moment, Princess. I'm going to turn your beautiful bottom a lovely shade of crimson. The heat coming from your skin will only be eclipsed by the fire in your core." Three more swats in rapid success sent fire racing over her skin, and for the first time, Cat wondered if she would be able to tolerate sixteen more. By the time she'd made it halfway through the punishment, Cat's entire body was heating as her mind turned off. There was nothing but an odd sense of distance between her and what was happening to her, and the disconnection was making it feel as if she was floating outside her body.

"It's subspace, Princess, the sweet space where your brain is so flooded with endorphins, the line between pain and pleasure no longer exists. It's a special part of your mind where you can let your mind float without worry or fear because it's a place you don't ordinarily care to go." Catalina had heard of subspace but wasn't sure she would have made the connection until later... probably a lot later. When she opened her mouth to speak, the only sound she was able to make was so garbled, she knew he couldn't have possibly understood how confusing it was to teeter between pleasure and pain. His words had to mean something, but for the life of her, she couldn't piece together where they should lead her.

Catalina remembered hearing subs talking about sub-space in the club's opulent locker room but hadn't thought she would ever be able to let go enough to experience it herself. The nature of her contract work meant there weren't many people she trusted implicitly and even fewer situations where she felt safe enough to let go.

"Your trust is the most valuable gift anyone has ever given me, Catalina. I'm looking forward to exploring your sexual needs. I'll help you open parts of yourself you have kept hidden from the rest of the world. There won't be a single part of yourself you won't feel safe sharing with me." Shifting on his lap, Cat wondered when Cooper had turned her over. How could she have been so lost in the moment, she'd failed to note a shift in position? "Have you forgotten we are mated, Princess? According to everything I've learned, genetics now dictate a deeper level of trust." Blinking at him, Cat wondered when he'd lost his fucking mind—she couldn't tell him... wait, what was it she couldn't share? "I suggest you do not give voice to those thoughts, Catalina. I'm not sure your tender backside can take any more swats just now."

No, Sherlock, I don't think my ass will ever be able to take any more. Hell, I doubt I'll be able to sit down for several days. Fucking hell, how am I going to work?

She knew how to block her thoughts since she'd been doing it most of her life. Hell, blocking was a survival skill when you had a younger brother who could read everyone's thoughts. The problem was remembering to put up those shields.

Goddess help her, first Israel, then Luke Grayson, her brother-in-law... and now Cooper. Damn it all to dusty doorknobs, Cam could read body language like it was his first language and her brother, Austin, was almost as perceptive. Now Cooper was stomping around in her thoughts, taking notes like a fricking court stenographer. Pretty soon, she wouldn't be able to hide anything, and everyone would know the other names... wait, what names? Her head started to ache, so she pushed it all aside.

"Floating around in subspace was nice... actually, it was fu... dging spectacular, but it remains to be seen if it was worth the long-term price."

"Good save, and I'll be interested in hearing what you decide." Setting her on her feet, Cooper kept his hands wrapped around her hips until he was sure she was steady. Once he was on his feet, he surprised her by wrapping an arm around her shoulders and walking her into the small room she knew he'd been using as an office. "I want you to take a quick look at the architect's blueprints. The designer also sent a slideshow for us to review. If there are any changes you want to make, now is the time."

Was he serious? He wanted her to review his remodeling plans... naked? He'd just paddled her into a stupor, and she was supposed to know what color throw pillows would look good on a damned sofa? The man might be her mate, but it seemed the DNA shift shaved off several critical IQ points. At this rate, Cooper would need to become a bit more officially retired than he was now. No one took Cam Barnes's *retirement* seriously, and she doubted Cooper's would get any more consideration.

Stepping into the office, Catalina was surprised to see a man's shirt draped over the back of the single office chair. Wrapping it around her shoulders, Cooper shook his head when she started to push a button through the hole. Pushing her hands aside, he buttoned a single small white disc in the center before pulling her onto his lap, chuckling when she hissed in pain. They spent the next hour looking at plans for a remodeling project she worried would take a decade to complete. When she expressed concern for the timeline rather than the scope of the project, he nodded.

"I agree, it's a damned ambitious plan, but I think you're going to be surprised how quickly it's wrapped up." She started to argue but thought better of it, deciding to hear him out. "We're fortunate to have a safe place to stay until we finish the investigation of your kidnapping. Cam and CeCe's guest house is as secure as this building and probably more secure than your workroom."

"Wait. You don't expect me to stop working and lounge around the pool, do you? If that's the case, you have me confused with someone else, mixed up a woman I don't even know." His chuckle surprised her, the vibration of his chest against her side igniting a fire in her core.

COOPER THOUGHT SHE was going to push through the memory block. He'd felt the lance of pain as it ricocheted around inside Catalina's head when she tried to pull the memory to the surface. Jesus, Joseph, and sweet Mother Mary, no wonder she wasn't willing to push herself past the pain—it was excruciating. Making a note to look for a private hypnotist, he wondered if waiting for Catalina to remember the information on her own was doing more harm than good.

Looking at the plans for the remodel was a good distraction. Catalina only made a couple of small changes. He'd laughed when she'd quietly vetoed the splashes of green the designer used. Cat's explanation had been simple, "Green is for tractors, grass, and trees."

Noting the changes and forwarding them to the contractor and design team, Cooper refocused his attention on the woman sitting on his lap. Tension rolled off her in waves despite the crushing fatigue he knew she was fighting. Smiling to himself, he wondered if she'd noticed many of their personal effects were missing. He'd given the movers permission to start, shocked by how much they'd managed to get finished in just a few hours. Shifting so he could look directly into her tired eyes, he opened his mouth to speak but closed it quickly when she shook her head.

"I'm tired of everyone walking on eggshells, pretending they are sparing my feelings, and treating me like I'm going to break." Cooper wasn't surprised she'd noticed. Hell, he'd known this was coming but hadn't expected it this soon. "It isn't your name or Cam's I'm struggling with, Cooper. Anyone with an IQ over room temperature would know I'd do anything to protect you and Cam." Okay, he'd be lying if he said she hadn't shocked him. They'd all been tiptoeing around for weeks, and she'd known all along their names were on the list?

"It has to be something or someone else, but who or what? I've never worked closely with any other agents." She was right, the reason Cat had been so successful was her distance from the Agency. As a jewelry designer, she'd been free to cross not only political borders but the invisible cultural boundaries as well.

"Have you considered the elusive name might not be an agent?" He'd spoken the words without taking time to think about how they might sound or think through how the question might affect her. She launched herself off his lap with such power and speed, he got a firsthand look at the shifter she kept concealed just beneath the surface. Pacing the length of the room, Catalina's grace was a thing of beauty. She didn't turn when she reached the end of the wall of windows—his new mate pivoted with the sleek style he usually associated with dancers.

"Thanks for the compliments. I'll attribute my ability to move at all to being genetically enhanced to heal at an accelerated rate." When he didn't comment, she froze in her tracks to turn, drilling him with a stare so intense, Cooper swore it felt like a slap. "My ass. I'm talking about my ass. If I wasn't a shifter, my ass would be so sore, I'd be moving at a snail's pace." Her response was so unexpected, Cooper couldn't hold back his bark of laughter. Hell, she was right, but then many submissives would have safe-worded out before reaching subspace.

"I'm amused by your repeated use of the word ass, Princess."

"It's an anatomical description, so it doesn't count as cursing." She hadn't missed a beat responding. Her lightning-fast mind was only one of the things he loved about her.

"Point taken, and for what it's worth, I'm glad you aren't suffering any long-term pain. I'll also take this opportunity to remind you safewords are in place for a reason. You will never be penalized for using it. A scene that works today might not work a month or a year from now. There are many reasons things change, and I don't want you to ever hesitate to slow things down if you need to or call a halt to the entire scene if it's too much for you."

Emotional triggers could change over time. Cooper had heard more than one story about a submissive who pushed through a scene simply because it hadn't been a problem before. Continuing with a scene when it was causing emotional harm went against every aspect of BDSM's guiding tenet. It wasn't safe, nor did it qualify as sane or consensual.

Since submissives are by nature pleasers, they often put their needs on the backburner, sacrificing what they knew was in their best interest, time and time again. He didn't expect it would ever be an issue with Catalina, but he wasn't going to pass up an opportunity to remind her.

COOPER WOKE UP to the soft rumbling of thunder in the distance and smiled. Texas weather was often unpredictable, confounding the forecasters, but thankfully, they'd gotten it right this time—unlike yesterday when they'd predicted storms, and it had been sunny and clear. It didn't matter how much he traveled, it always took time for his body to reset to a new time zone. He didn't consider it jet lag because he didn't have any of the swamping fatigue, sleep disruptions, or stomach disorders other people complained about. It was more about his body slowly shifting back to what most people considered a normal circadian cycle.

"For the love of all things sacred, stop thinking so loud. It's too early for all this chatter." Cooper chuckled as he pushed the hair away from her face.

"Still not a morning person, Princess?" It always amused him how predictably her body clock operated. No matter what time zone they were in, Cat was a night owl, preferring to work until just before sunrise, then sleep until late morning. More often than not, she skidded into the hotel's brunch buffet moments after it closed. She usually spent the next ten minutes feeding the concierge a sob-story, her performances often worthy of an Oscar nomination. After stumbling upon the mini production by accident, Cooper made a point to be in the restaurant every time thereafter. After a particularly stunning performance, he'd applauded, which infuriated her.

"Please, I'm begging you. Stop. Thinking. So. Loud." When she made a grab for a pillow, he laughed out loud. There wasn't any way to muffle telepathic noise.

"I agree, staying in bed at this point should include a lot

more than *thinking*." Before she could voice an argument, Cooper flipped her over and pinned her hands over her head. A glint of mischief was shining in her eyes, but he knew she wouldn't attempt a countermove. She wouldn't be able to escape, but he decided to make certain she understood the benefits of submitting far outweighed any small sliver of pride she would find in a token protest.

"Don't move, Princess. I'm in the mood to play, and since you're awake anyway…" He felt more than heard her quick snort of derision, but she wisely kept whatever wisecrack was dancing on the tip of her tongue to herself. It didn't escape his attention, she was also shielding her thoughts, a wise move considering the circumstance. Pressing soft kisses over her eyes, Cooper knew she had understood the implied command to keep her eyes closed. Kissing his way down the side of her face and following the line of her jaw, Cooper grinned when goosebumps raced over her skin.

Pressing his tongue against the rapid pulse pounding at the base of her throat, Cooper felt her heart rate kick up. Damn, the woman was so responsive, it was like tossing gas on the fire of his desire. The farther down her body his lips moved, the shallower her breathing became. By the time he reached the smooth skin above her sex, Cat's scent was thick in the air. Learning about all the physical enhancements that would follow mating hadn't fully prepared him for the reality. Her pussy had always tasted sweeter than any other woman he'd ever had, but this was something so much more intense, he knew there was no way he could ever explain it. The first lick through her slick folds sent the taste of wild honey bursting over his tastebuds.

"Fucking perfect. You taste so good, I may spend the entire morning feasting on you and say to hell with the brunch I ordered." The muscles beneath his hands stiffened, and he wasn't disappointed when pictures of her favorites drifted through his mind. Evidently, it was harder for her to shield her thoughts when he pushed her closer to release. "It's going to be a tough call, my sweet mate. Everything about you makes my cock ache to claim what is mine. On the other hand, I can feel your hunger, and those pictures of sausage and bacon in cream gravy pouring over steaming butter biscuits are giving me a taste of an entirely different kind of hunger."

"Please. I need to feel you inside me." *I need to know you still want me... that the woman you found in that dirty cell isn't the one you see when you look at me.*

Cooper couldn't believe what he'd just *heard.*

"You know what I see every time I look at you, Princess?" She stiffened, but he refused to apologize for listening in on her thoughts or coddle her with hollow platitudes. "I see the strongest woman I've ever known—a survivor fighting her way back from an experience so horrific, it would have left most people shattered. I see a woman who has put everything on the line time and time again to do what she knew was the right thing. Every scar is a testament to your survival. Every nightmare gives me a chance to hold you, sharing my strength until yours is renewed. I see a woman who expects too much from herself, asks too little of those around her, and has forgotten it's okay to lean on the people who love her."

Watching Cat's eyes fill with tears as she tried in vain

to blink them away melted his resolve to affirm without cosseting her. Sliding his bare flesh along her satin-smooth skin, he moved back up until they were once again face to face. Kissing away Catalina's salty tears, he knew she didn't see herself the way he did, but he planned to keep telling her what he saw until she believed him.

"I'm humbled, Ace." He smiled at her use of the nickname she'd given him when they first met. He'd always pretended to be annoyed but was, in fact, secretly amused. Cooper had known then what she'd refused to admit for far too long—Catalina Adler was his from the moment he saw her walking across campus. It didn't matter that she had already been recruited by the Agency months earlier, and he had been assigned to review her security clearance. Everything about her impressed him, but it was a midnight run in a nearby park that sealed the deal.

"Oh. My. Freaking. Goddess. You saw me shift?"

Damn, he really was going to have to talk to Brigitte or one of the Adler wives about blocking.

Chapter Six

SITTING ON HER deck stark naked, rain pounding down on the awning covering her small outdoor space, was a surprisingly sensual experience. Piecing on her favorite brunch foods made the entire scene seem decadently overindulgent, but she didn't care. Her position protected her from the stinging raindrops falling so hard, they'd made her flinch before Cooper pulled her chair closer to the building.

"I love the weather in Texas. It changes so often, you never have a chance to get bored." Cooper's deep voice resonated with admiration, and she smiled when she realized he was speaking more to himself than to her.

"True, and rains like this lift my mood by positively charging the ions in the air. So many people scoff, claiming it's a theory or some kind of new-age nonsense, but it's science. I think I was in the third or fourth grade when the teacher talked about how rain could positively charge the ions in the air. Holy Hannah, I was so excited to finally be able to relate the way I felt to a scientific fact. So much of my life was centered on magic and other things I wasn't allowed to talk to outsiders about, it was limiting. Finding some common ground was exhilarating. Unfortunately, we started moving a lot not long after that, and our parents started homeschooling us."

Cooper was watching her so closely, Cat swore he was studying her like she was a lab rat. His unrepentant grin let her know she was thinking too loud again. *Damn, I really need to pay attention.*

"You are not a lab rat, Princess. I was simply hoping you would keep talking. You rarely share anything about your childhood, and I was enjoying the glimpse into that time of your life."

She stared at him, surprised to realize she appeared so closed off. In fact, her early life had been filled with extensive world travel and educational experiences that shaped the woman she'd become.

Cooper shifted his position until their chairs were fully facing one another. Leaning back, with his elbows resting on the arms of the chair and fingers steepled under his chin, Cooper gave her a lecherous grin. Cat felt the energy around them kick up and knew the dynamic had shifted. They didn't need a code word. She was always able to sense when their interaction changed to a D/s scene.

"Show me what is mine, Princess. Scoot your delectable ass forward, lean back, and spread your beautiful legs. Hook your knees over the arms of your chair. I want to see every delicious bit."

It took a couple of seconds for her to process his words. She probably looked like an idiot sitting outside stark naked, eating so much, she was closing in on a carb-coma and blinking like a deer caught in the headlights. Her brain finally kicked into gear, and she set aside the pastry in her hand. Getting into position wasn't difficult, but she was surprised by how vulnerable she felt.

When she heard a noise from the patio below hers, Catalina started to move. Her outdoor space had been designed to provide the best possible view, and she loved the all-glass enclosure. The suite below hers was only used when Adler Oil hosted out-of-town guests, so she hadn't given the glass floor any thought.

"Stay still, Catalina. The couple using the guest suite has come to Austin to interview for positions at Adler Oil and have just returned from a visit to Prairie Winds. They are voyeurs and long-time members of the ShadowDance Club. Health concerns require a warmer climate, so they're hoping to move to Texas.' She started to look down, but a subtle shake of his head reminded her to stay focused on her Dom. It had been so long since they'd played, Catalina was struggling to remember the rules. Cooper wasn't overly strict, but one of his hard and fast rules was keeping her eyes on him unless otherwise instructed.

"I have a couple of gifts for you. We'll make sure they are in place before we proceed." Cooper's pause was deliberate—he was giving her a chance to use her safe-word, but Cat already knew she wouldn't. She was a bit of an exhibitionist and was thrilled to know they were being watched with appreciation rather than judgment. The velvet box Cooper set on the table was from her store. When had he managed to make a purchase she didn't know about? Flipping up the lid, the rat palmed whatever was inside before kneeling in front of her.

"I can hear all those questions, Princess. Let's do a little quality control experiment today, shall we?" Opening his hand, she saw a clit ring she'd designed. She liked to tell customers the small gold ring was a cross between their grandmother's clip earrings and their grandfather's wood-working clamps. "I want to see how you play with your pretty pussy when we're apart. Slide your fingers through those slick folds, get them nice and wet, then lose yourself for a few seconds... but don't come."

Her hand had already been moving in anticipation of the release she craved, but his admonishment to not come made her freeze. For a few seconds, she wasn't sure he was serious. The time they had together was always so limited, orgasm denial had never been a part of their play. How was she supposed to hold back? Cripes, didn't he know she wasn't one of those delayed gratification people? A split second before she opened her mouth to tell him what she thought of his plan, somewhere in the very back of her mind, Cat's subconscious registered an odd echo. Before she could process what it was, the glass beside her splin-tered into a spiderweb of fractures. If her brother hadn't insisted on impact-resistant glass, the shot would have gone into her upper thigh. Whoever pulled the trigger wasn't trying to kill her, but they damned well planned to make certain she was slowed down for the foreseeable future.

Catalina's training kicked in, and she was on the floor before Cooper finished shouting at the couple below them to get back inside. Cat saw them scramble out of harm's way and wondered how fast they'd be packed up and head back to Colorado. Damn, Austin was going to be pissed she'd screwed this up for him.

Are you fucking kidding me? Some jackass is taking potshots at you, and you're worried about what big brother is going to say about a couple of job applicants? Hell, one of those applicants was a Green Beret, not much chance he'll be frightened off by a shot aimed at someone else.

Great, just what she needed, her brother's voice bouncing around in her head while she was naked. Damn, this shit was getting old.

"Get dressed. We're moving a little sooner than planned. I think this was supposed to be a snatch and grab."

"Why would they aim for my thigh? It makes their first order of business providing medical care." Once inside, she stood and turned back to the sliding glass doors. The floor to ceiling glass would protect them from anything short of a military attack, and she wanted to scan the neighboring rooftops. The Adler Oil building was the tallest for several blocks around, so there was little chance the shot came from above.

"Catalina. Focus, please."

Blinking in surprise, she wondered how long Cooper had been speaking to her. Where the hell was her head? That sort of distraction got agents killed. She needed to pull her head out of her ass… quickly.

"If I hadn't tilted my head down looking at your slick fold, the shot would have drilled my temple, Princess. Whoever took the shot overcorrected, and the second attempt hit the glass." Shit, that's why she'd heard an echo. It was embarrassing to admit she hadn't heard the first shot.

"I don't know who we're dealing with because there are too many things that don't add up. They know enough to take me out before trying to grab you." He was right. Anyone who knew anything at all about her had to be aware of their relationship. They'd know Cooper would protect her at all costs. "The fucker obviously isn't a pro." Cat agreed. Pros don't miss, and on the off chance something interfered with their first shot, they damned well didn't overcorrect. "Get dressed, Cat. Pack one bag. Someone will bring the rest."

Why did she feel like she was watching the world through a fog? Sounds were muffled and spinning. *Fuck a duck. Why is the room spinning?* She had the vague sense of falling before a distant curse filled the air, followed by nothing but silent darkness.

IF COOPER HADN'T been listening in on Catalina's thoughts, he wouldn't have realized she was fading until it was too late. Hell, the way it was, he'd barely gotten to her in time to catch her in his arms a few inches above the hardwood floor. If she wasn't naked, he'd have just set aside the need to pack a bag and walk straight out the door. Wrapping the soft throw from the back of the sofa around her, Cooper settled Cat then started making calls. He wasn't sure how long he'd been on the phone when he felt the air around him crackle with electricity.

"Good, you are finally mated; that will help."

Spinning around, Cooper yanked his weapon from the back of his jeans and tried to conceal his surprise, finding Brigitte Stafford standing behind him. Damn, didn't she know how dangerous it was to sneak up on an agent? Fucking hell, he could have shot her. Her snort of disgust pulled his attention back to the moment.

"As if. I believe you'll find your bullets in your pocket,

Deputy Fife."

Cooper shook his head when he realized there was a noticeable weight in his shirt pocket. Checking his weapon, Cooper sighed when he discovered it was, indeed, unloaded. Jesus, Joseph, and sweet Mother Mary, he was never going to get used to the ways of the magic world. They seemed to operate under an entirely different set of rules, and he still hadn't been given a damned copy. Cameron Barnes might be his best friend and mentor, but Cooper wasn't sure he fully understood the other man's obsession with all things magic. Hell, from what Cooper could see, it convinced shifters and wizards they were protected when it didn't seem that cut and dried to him.

"You were the target. I'm always shocked by nonmagicals who seem to believe there is some logic in their roundabout plans."

"Perhaps that's because they don't have the ability to unload a weapon without touching it." Crossing his arms over his chest, Cooper leaned against the wall hoping the casual pose would convince them both he wasn't rattled.

"Pish posh. Nonmagicals have too many rules."

"I don't suppose you caught the son of a bitch who signed his own death warrant by taking potshots at us?"

"Cranky because he interrupted your scene?" Her tone was taunting, but Brigitte's eyes sparkled with amusement.

"Fucking A." Cooper was pissed about the interruption, but more than that, he was furious the incident elicited such a strong response from Catalina. She was finally sleeping better, experiencing fewer nightmares, and her appetite was slowly returning—no doubt a good chunk of that progress was now as shattered as the damned balcony glass.

"I'll help you get her out to Cam's. CeCe has agreed to check her out while the three of us chat." Cooper wanted to roll his eyes. If he wasn't convinced the woman had Cat's best interest at heart, he would send her on her merry way. Catalina was sitting up but still looked dazed when he turned to check on her. Spotting Gigi, Cat shook her head and chuckled.

"I'm not riding your broomstick out to Cam's."

"Spoilsport." It was easy to see there was genuine affection as well as mutual respect between the two women. "I promise to ride in a regular car as long as you aren't the one driving. Damn, girl, your driving is on a whole new level of terrifying. I think you share Cleveland's penchant for speed without having his skill set."

"Damn, Gigi, tell me what you really think." Getting to her feet, Cat seemed to be drawing strength from the air around her—it was fascinating to watch. "I swear your ruthless streak is growing at an alarming rate." Gigi shrugged, but Cooper saw the glint of concern in her eyes. If Brigitte was worried about Catalina's safety, they had bigger problems than how to get out to Cam and CeCe's. Cat stalked down the hall, muttering about the joys of incompetent assassins and crazy witches with pissy attitudes.

Cooper returned his attention to Gigi and felt his eyes go wide when Audric was standing beside her. What the hell? Didn't these people ever use the fucking door?

"Didn't you say they were mated? He seems awfully tense for somebody whose sex life should have suddenly improved exponentially." Audric's attempt to hide his amusement failed miserably, and Cooper was starting to wonder if he'd somehow been transported into the twilight zone. "Rod Serling was a remarkable actor. His ability to introduce our world to yours in a way that looked like entertainment was brilliant."

Shaking his head at the elderly wizard, Cooper wondered if Audric would allow Lakyn to interview him. His sister was an international best-selling romance author, but lately, she'd been talking about venturing into another genre.

"You're feeding his ego, Cooper. Damn, there'd be no living with him if your sister wrote a best-seller about his life." Gigi rolled her eyes, making certain everyone knew what she thought of the idea.

"Well, that's just insulting." Audric's mocking tone was amusing, but Cooper suspected he was probably a better actor than his phony act indicated. Cooper had to bite the inside of his cheek to keep from laughing at his lame attempt to appear indignant. Pasting on a smile intended to make him look honored, Audric added, "I'd love to speak with Lakyn. My lovely daughter has issued a challenge I can't possibly let go unmet. If she wants to fill the empty seat on the Council, she needs to learn the fine art of finesse." Cooper saw the sparks flying around the room and grinned. Damn, the physical enhancements of mating were fucking awesome.

CAMERON BARNES LEANED against the bedframe, watching his lovely submissive try to steady her breathing. He and

Carl had spun her up as far as they dared before stepping back, leaving her teetering on the edge of climax. Cecelia was amazing in every way imaginable, but there were times when she did so much for everyone else in her life, the brilliant surgeon ignored her own needs.

They needed to wrap up their scene, but the view was fucking spectacular and damned hard to give up. Their home was going to be teeming with people before long, and Cam wanted to ensure the lovely Dr. Barnes was well satisfied before their guests arrived. Grateful they'd blindfolded her, Cam gave Carl the signal to move to the head of the bed.

As the permanent third in their relationship, Carl Phillips was the only man Cam would ever allow in their bed. As a sexual dominant, Carl didn't submit to anyone but Cam—not ever. While Carl moved into position, Cam stepped forward to check CeCe's restraints one more time, making certain the fur-lined cuffs weren't cutting off her circulation.

"Any tingling or numbness, Pet?" He kept his voice low, knowing how much the deep timbre pulled his sub deeper into the scene.

"No, Sir." Her breathing was slow but shallow, and he could hear the underlying strain in her voice. He knew she was focused on listening for their movement—assessing each sound as she tried to anticipate what was coming. Cecelia was well-trained in the lifestyle, so she wouldn't ask what they had planned, but that didn't mean she wasn't going to gather any information she could. Brilliant minds like CeCe's functioned best when they were pulling together every available snippet of intel and assembling the pieces into something useful. The woman would have made one hell of an agent.

CeCe turned her head and licked her lips when Carl knelt on the bed beside her. Painting her lips with the pre-cum pearled at the tip of his cock, Carl's head fell back, the strain on his face easy to read.

"Open for me, baby. I'm going to fuck your mouth while your other master claims your sweet pussy." From Cam's position, he could see a fresh wash of cream seep from her depths push forward, coating her swollen labia. CeCe was gloriously responsive, and he loved the effect their words had on her. Watching her lips wrap around Carl's thick cock was hotter than hell, and he hoped the man could hold on long enough to enjoy what Cam had planned.

Grabbing a bottle of lube, Cam moved to the bed and smiled down at the scene before him. They'd already pushed pillows under her ass, so she was in the perfect position for the plundering he would give her. The clit ring Carl fitted over her sensitive bundle of nerves before their break highlighted the deep red berry Cam knew was throbbing with the need to be touched. Nodding to Carl, Cam watched him throw one long leg over their woman, straddling her chest, his testicles resting against the underside of her chin.

"That's it, Sweetness. Take me all the way to your throat and swallow every drop of the gift I'm going to give you." Cam smiled at Carl's back. The man was not only his friend but also his partner. Carl was known for his control, but the man was going to fill their sub with his seed when Cam slipped his fingers into the man's ass. They were cutting it close on time, and Cam was out of patience. Pushing himself balls deep in one thrust, feeling the walls of CeCe's vagina flexing and quivering around him was the closest thing to heaven Cam had ever experienced. Damn, he loved this woman more than life itself.

Smoothing his hand over Carl's back, Cam applied just enough pressure to let the man know what he wanted. One of the joys of a committed relationship was the ability to communicate with just a touch. Cam continued the slow thrusting pace he'd set, fucking their woman as Carl went to his hands and knees. His new position changed the angle of his cock sliding in and out of CeCe's mouth, and Cam chuckled when the petite vixen's nipples drew up into stiff peaks. She obviously sensed what was coming.

Pulling on a latex glove and lubing his fingers, Cam used one hand to open Carl's rear hole to his view. Pushing two fingers through the tight ring of muscles of Carl's anus, Cam watched goosebumps race over the man's back as his thrusts into CeCe's mouth accelerated. Rotating his hand until he found the spot he wanted to massage, Cam began thrusting with his hips, knowing it was going to be a race to the finish. Carl groaned as his muscles seized around Cam's fingers. CeCe's pussy went liquid around him, her vaginal muscles locking down so tight, it bordered on painful. His grunted command for them to come was a wasted effort, but what the hell, old habits die hard.

Yanking his hand free from Carl's tight hold, Cam pulled off the glove to grip his wife's hips with a hold tight enough he hoped would leave marks lasting a few hours. Damn, he loved knowing she wore the evidence of his passion under whatever clingy dress he found for her to wear. Within seconds, he followed them over the edge, grateful Carl had moved to CeCe's side so Cam could collapse against the soft pillows of her breasts.

"You two melted me. I'm a big pile of liquid goo. How am I supposed to check on Catalina when my leg muscles won't hold me up? Hell, my brain is only firing on half its blasted cylinders." CeCe's words might have been more amusing if Cam wasn't dealing with the same problem. When the front gate alarm sounded, Cam groaned. Carl shook his head and chuckled, moving from the bed to retrieve his phone. Checking the security feed to confirm the arrival of their first guests before opening the gate, Carl gave CeCe's nipple a quick tweak.

"Come on, you two. We have company." Carl was always the first to recover from their scenes, something Cam nor CeCe had never been able to understand. He'd told them once it was a mindset left over from his days as a Navy SEAL. "When you don't know if you will live to see another day, you don't want to waste time being numb." Cameron wasn't convinced his explanation was entirely accurate, but he didn't have anything better, so he'd wisely kept quiet.

After what was equivalent to a walkthrough shower, Cam dressed quickly and made his way downstairs to his office, stunned to find it teeming with people. Hell, it hadn't taken him that long. How did he manage to miss the arrival of so many visitors?

"Did we interrupt anything?" Brigitte Stafford's taunting tone was only eclipsed by the huge grin on her face.

"Yes, as a matter of fact, you did. I expected better from a fellow Dominant, particularly one with the magical ability to know, waiting another hour would have been perfect. You nearly got a lesson in the lifestyle you wouldn't forget anytime soon." The pink stain over the witch's face made him wonder if there wasn't a submissive's heart hiding behind all the bravado. How interesting.

Chapter Seven

CATALINA LEANED BACK in the leather chair, watching the fire, and sipping the wine CeCe handed her. Dr. Cecelia Barnes might be one of the world's most in-demand pediatric surgeons, but sitting cross-legged on the floor, the dark-haired beauty looked more like a teenager than a successful physician.

"Thanks for checking on me. I'm grateful some well-meaning control freak—no need to be specific and name names—didn't try to fly my happy ass to freaking Mayo Clinic for a four-day exam. I swear there must be a class at Prairie Winds to train Doms in the fine art of paranoia." CeCe nodded and took another swig of wine, frowning at her glass as if it was draining itself.

"I'm not a primary care provider, and you're a bit over the age of my usual patients." Tipping her glass up to glaring at the bottom, she muttered a curse. "Damn, this glass must be leaking."

"Hey, that wasn't a 'dis about my age, was it? Because if it was, I'd have to turn you into a toad or something." Catalina giggled when she realized how slurred her words sounded. Glancing at the wine bottle sitting on the small table beside her. "Hey, who drank all our wine?"

84

"What? Well, damn, when did that happen? I can't believe we didn't notice someone helping themselves to our stolen goods. Frack, that's one of Cam's favorites, too. He isn't going to be happy when he sees the whole bottle is gone." CeCe scooted over to pick up the bottle, holding it over her head to look in the bottom as if the deep red liquid was somehow being concealed by the label. "Damn, would you look at that? Not even a drop left. Amazing."

"It was good... too bad we were robbed. That really sucks. You can't trust anybody these days." Catalina tried to focus on the bottle but was having trouble figuring out which of the three she saw was the real one. "Hey, hold that still so I can read the label."

"Still? It's sitting on the table. I'm not moving it. Maybe we're having an earthquake because the whole room seems to be moving." CeCe reached out, planting her palms flat on the floor, grinning, "There, that's better. I fixed it. You're welcome." A fit of giggles moved over her in a crashing wave, nearly making her fall over. "Tell me how you learned to turn into a wolf. Did you get a handbook? Did you have to get a license, like you do, to drive? There must be some protocol or procedure."

"Say what? You're not a proctologist." Catalina looked at her friend and shuddered. "No offense, but I'm not into that sort of thing."

"I don't care anything about your ass, Catalina. Protocol... you know, rules about how something is supposed to be done."

"Damn, CeCe, you are such a geek. No, wait, that's my brother-in-law... umm, shit. What's his name? The one married to B."

"Luke? Isn't he related to somebody we know?"

"Yeah, but I'm not going to think about that... it's dangerous. He dials in too easily. He's an employee. No, he's an emperor. No. For duck's sake, what's the word?"

"Empath." Cooper's deep voice came from somewhere over the shoulder. When Catalina turned to look, she fell out of her chair. Her unladylike tumble made them burst into another fit of giggles.

"Did you hear what you said? For duck's sake? Oh, that's great... I should remember that. Maybe I'll write it down. If we didn't see who stole the wine, there's a good chance I might not remember that little ditty tomorrow." CeCe looked over at Cat and frowned. "You fell out of the chair. That's a shame 'cause it took you several tries to climb all the way up there. Are you okay? I'm a doctor, you know. If you have something broken, I could fix it. Maybe not tonight, but eventually."

COOPER STARED AT the two women on the floor in front of the fire, shaking his head. "This has to be some sort of record. How did they manage to get so sloshed in such a short time?"

"Well, they did drink an entire bottle of wine." Carl Phillips stood between Cooper and Cam, a huge smile on his face.

"A very expensive bottle of wine, I might add. Hell, you have to give them credit for pulling one of my prized bottles out of the cellar." Cam shook his head in mock disgust, but there wasn't any hint of anger in his voice.

"Come on, let's get them to bed. Carl, you take care of our woman, and I'll show our guests to their temporary home. Interviewing Catalina tonight would be an exercise in futility."

"Did he say he exercises for fertility? I'd be interested in hearing how that works. I saw something on the internet once about women who stand on their heads after sex, hoping gravity will help all the little swimmers find their mark." Cat frowned at the crowd standing around her before turning to CeCe. "Hey, how many men do you have, anyway? There's a whole group of them up there, and only three are mine."

CeCe's eyes narrowed as she tried to focus. It was all Cooper could do to keep a straight face when the pretty brunette tried to make her eyes lock onto the three of them.

"I've got two... but honest to God, I don't know which two are real. It would be a lot easier to figure out if they would all just stand the hell still. Frack, they are weaving around like a bunch of frat boys on a fender."

"Fender? That can't be right. I don't think that's the right word. Isn't a fender some sort of car part?"

"Oh, yeah. Well, it's something like that. When I was in college, frat boys were always coming up with some reason to get wasted... you know, like *it's Thursday, we should celebrate.*"

Cooper saw Carl roll his eyes as he stepped forward to scoop Cecelia into his arms. "Come on, Sweetness. Let's get you up to bed before you say something that's going to get you into even more trouble." CeCe was giggling as Carl carried her out of the room and up the winding staircase.

"Your turn, Princess. There is no reason to ask you anything tonight." Picking her up, he noted she was still underweight. Frowning, he wondered how the hell he'd failed to notice how slight she felt cradled in his arms. Making a mental note to make sure she ate regularly, he followed Cam into the attached guest quarters. Cam's deep chuckle drew Cooper's attention.

"I'd like to be frustrated with the two of them, but the truth is, they've both had a rough time of it lately, and I'm glad they let off some of the steam where we could keep an eye on them."

Cooper agreed and grinned as he headed down the short hall to the bedroom. Covering her with a quilt, Cooper walked back into the living room and laughed.

"If she wasn't a shifter, I'd be worried about how she's going to feel in the morning, but I've seen how quickly her body metabolizes alcohol. She'll be fine in a couple of hours. In the meantime, I'm sticking close to make sure she doesn't manage to get her sweet ass into more trouble."

"Trouble does seem to have a way of finding her lately. I'm beginning to think her growing magic is pulling trouble from the shadows." Cam's words were likely more accurate than any of them knew. Audric and Gigi had alluded to as much during the earlier strategy session in Cam's office. "We need her functional for several reasons." Chuckling, Cam started for the door, then paused. Turning to look at Cooper, Cam's expression lost all traces of humor.

"Whoever tried to take you out wasn't a pro, but even fools get lucky, eventually. I'm putting my money on a magical, trying to throw us off. Be careful. Underestimating an adversary because he failed to kill you the first time would be a whole new level of arrogance. If mating with Catalina is bringing you newfound magical abilities, we need to utilize those skills while keeping the information under our hats. This is going to be a high stakes game, Cooper. Don't show your hand too early."

"Hey, it's darker than the inside of a cat in here. Who turned out the damned lights? Didn't Cam pay the power bill? Those bastards at the power company get off on throwing switches. I hate it when that happens. Power-hungry power company... yeah, there's some irony for ya." Catalina's grumbling voice filled the small apartment. The grin spreading over Cam's face made him look much younger than Cooper knew him to be. In the back of his mind, Cooper sent up a silent prayer, the man would smile more now that he was backing even farther away from his former employer. Honestly, there was a part of him that wondered if either of them would ever be truly free of their former lives. The distinctive sound of a click sounded from the bedroom, followed by a flood of light into the hall.

"Oh. Well, there's a coincidence for you. Speaking of throwing switches, it looks like I just needed to find the right one. No worries about the honorable men and women at the power company or Cam's financial state." Cam's snort of laughter as he turned and walked out was mild compared to Cooper's bark of laughter.

Damn, Catalina was as entertaining now as she was the first time they'd worked together. He'd been impressed as hell by her analysis of seemingly unrelated facts and her innate ability to discern the needs of people—her beauty and wit had been bonuses. His only issue with the skilled agent was her driving.

"What's wrong with my driving? I'm an excellent driver. I've never had an accident, and I haven't had a speeding ticket in years. You want to get all grinchy about somebody's driving, go after Paris. She's always had a serious need for speed."

A need Cooper knew Paris's husband, a sheriff near their home outside Boston, was working diligently to curb. Her shouted response came from the master bath. Turning that way, Cooper couldn't help but wonder what she'd gotten into. *Hell, who knows what disaster awaits.* Walking down the short hall, Cooper found his very inebriated mate walking out of the bathroom, gloriously naked and dripping wet.

"Catalina, you forgot to dry off after your shower." She blinked several times, tipping her head to the side as if she were trying to decipher what language he was speaking. "Princess, did you use a towel after your shower?"

"Shit, I knew I forgot something." Pivoting on her heel, she made her way back to the bathroom in a few long strides. Returning to the bedroom a few seconds later, a towel wrapped around her head like a turban, her gloriously naked body was still on full display and still dripping wet. When he laughed, she stomped her foot. "What now?" She flinched when the hand she'd waved dramatically in the air hit the edge of the dresser. "Damn it, that hurt." Glaring at him, he pointed her finger in his direction. "This is your fault."

"My fault? How did you arrive at that misguided conclusion, Princess?"

"I wouldn't be in this pickle if you hadn't made me fall in love with you. Nobody cared about my little piece of the magic pie until you came along. I lost all control after I met you. And then I mated with you, and now you are going to be a target, too." When he stared at her in surprise, she didn't just roll her eyes—the damned woman rolled her whole head.

"Oh, puuuhhhleese. You think just because I drank a little… okay, more than a little… probably more like *a lot* of wine, doesn't mean I don't know up from sideways. Alcohol doesn't keep me from being perceptive, although it does seem to affect my ability to remember little things."

"Like drying off after a shower?"

"You're not going to let that go, are you?" He flashed her a grin, he knew was every bit as sinister-looking as he intended it to be. "No, I can see you are going to run this into the ground. I'll bet you were a real pain in the ass as a brother." He raised a brow in question. Lakyn had been so much younger, the two of them hadn't experienced many of the usual sibling challenges and rivalries most brothers and sisters faced. "Don't give me that phony confused look. I'll bet you can still name every bad grade Lakyn got in school… what subject it was… who her teacher was, and what your parents said when you told them to check her bookbag." She was right, but not for the reason she assumed. Cooper had a photographic memory, rarely forgot any detail, and certainly not anything related to his baby sister.

"My sister is whip-smart. Any poor grade she received was because she wasn't applying herself." The damned woman standing in front of him had the audacity to burst out laughing.

"I knew it. Lakyn should be nominated for sainthood.

At least my brothers spread their 'monitoring for your own good' bullshit around." *Did she seriously just use air-quotes?* "And they didn't have the excuse of taking on the role of parents, except for Paris, so the rest of us didn't hesitate to tell them to piss-off."

"Lakyn only made *that* mistake once. Hanging upside down by one ankle over the banister convinced her being disrespectful wasn't in her best interest." He wasn't going to mention his mouthy sister had been sixteen at the time. The only other time he'd been tempted to paddle the little imp's ass had been when she'd walked in on a scene in his living room. He'd suspected she knew about his lifestyle, but having it confirmed was damned uncomfortable.

Watching as Catalina processed what he'd said as well as the thoughts he hadn't shared aloud, Cooper hoped like hell she wouldn't start asking questions. The last thing he wanted to waste time doing when she was standing naked in front of him was to engage in a heart-to-heart discussion about former lovers. He didn't want to do it now... hell, he would probably never want to talk about all the mistakes he'd made over the years.

"Not going there, Ace. I'm not one of those women who wants to know all the women you fucked. Not my circus, not my... well, I guess you are my monkey now, but you weren't then so..." He could see goosebumps moving over her skin and shook his head when her nipples drew up into the tightest points he'd ever seen.

"Are you cold, Princess? If you had used the towel to dry off before wrapping your hair, you wouldn't be turning into a popsicle. Come on, let's get you a shirt."

"Thought you were all about having your subs sleep

naked?" So, it seemed she had been interested enough in his history to do at least a cursory investigation. He didn't want to think about what she'd likely discovered.

"Until we figure out who is trying to take you away from me, I want you to be ready to run at a moment's notice. I know shifting will shred whatever you are wearing, but what if you aren't able to shift for some reason?" Feeling vulnerable would be too distracting, and he didn't even want to contemplate what would happen if her captor ran face-first into an emotional trigger. Handing her one of his shirts, Cooper helped her slip into a finely spun cotton dress shirt and smiled down at her.

"You look adorable, Princess. The last woman I saw wearing anything of mine was Lakyn. I don't even want to think about how many of my shirts the brat got away with." His kid sister always told him they made her feel like he was close even when he'd been gone on missions. Hell, there'd been times he wasn't sure he'd get back to her, and those moments were all it took for him to overlook her raids on his closet.

Taking her hand, Cooper led Catalina to the small living room, settling her on the loveseat with a throw over her lap before moving to the kitchen. Five minutes later, he returned, carrying a tray of finger foods and bottled water.

"Either you planned ahead, or you're much faster in the kitchen than I am—of course, that wouldn't actually be difficult." Cooper laughed out loud at her admission.

"I planned ahead. It may surprise you, but I can cook. I learned because I got tired of takeout and frozen dinners. I hoped it would inspire Lakyn to follow suit, but that didn't go as well as I would have liked. I'm grateful her men like to cook, so my niece and nephew aren't eating food their mama shakes out of a bag and pops into a toaster oven. When she is writing, the last thing on her mind is cooking... hell, her husbands are lucky if they can get her to stop to eat."

"My mom made sure all my brothers could cook, and dad taught the girls how to change tires and the oil in our cars. When my dad found out I wanted to make jewelry and needed to learn how to weld, he took the evening class with me." Cooper glanced down to see Cat rolling the fabric of the shirt's tail between her fingers. He knew the small tell was the only habit she'd never been able to break. Now that she'd been forced into retirement from covert work, he hoped she wouldn't feel the need to hide so much of herself.

"Did I ever tell you I met your parents?" Cat jolted in surprise at the simple question, her wide eyes and gaping mouth all the answer he needed. Plunging ahead without waiting for her response, Cooper continued, "They saw through me within the first two minutes, knew our meeting hadn't been accidental, and recognized it for the security check it was. The first time I met Lilly West, she reminded me of your mom—not in looks, but her take no prisoners, mama bear attitude. Your dad was more introspective. He sat back—watching and listening. His questions were much more personal."

"Personal? How?"

Cooper had known when he admitted meeting her parents this was the direction the conversation would head. Now that they were mated, he felt more confident revealing how much had taken place without her knowing.

"While your mom was focused on how the agency planned to utilize your magical ability, your dad was more concerned with my romantic interest in you. He wanted my assurance your heart was safe with me."

"Oh, geez, how embarrassing. It's like the 'what are your intentions' speeches from the old days. There wasn't any talk of doweries, was there? That would be too much... you probably asked him for a cow and a couple of ducks, didn't you?" Cooper knew her attempt to make light of the situation hid deep-seated insecurity. Cat's lack of self-esteem baffled anyone who knew her. She was stunningly beautiful, brilliant, witty, loyal, and talented, yet there was a small part of her that didn't feel like she was worthy of the gifts the Universe had bestowed upon her.

"I didn't ask him for anything other than his trust. I assured him I would protect you with my life, and your heart would always be safe in my keeping. At the time, I didn't know all the details of mating, but as it turns out, my assurances lined up perfectly." He took her hand in his, giving her fingers a quick squeeze before pulling them to his lips. "Your mom was a force of nature. Even with my lack of understanding at that point, I could feel the energy pulsing around her. I might not have understood the significance, but there was no mistaking the power."

"She was very powerful, more than any of us knew." He could hear respect and sadness in her voice.

"Why do I hear the word *but* you failed to tack onto the end of that statement?" Cooper's question elicited a small smile from the woman he was going to spend the rest of his life loving.

"My dad wasn't the strongest magical, but his ability to

connect with people, to understand what they needed, what it took to make them feel whole... made him more special than magic ever could."

Seeing the unshed tears in Catalina's eyes as she spoke about her dad made Cooper realize it didn't matter that she'd been considered an adult when her parents were killed. There would always be a little girl inside her who'd lost her daddy. He knew from experience the pain never far below the surface. Smoothing his fingers along the under-side of her chin brought his lovely mate back to the moment.

"Your dad called me a few days before their accident." Cooper watched as Catalina's eyes widened. He knew the Adler siblings had heard similar stories at the time of the car wreck, and those painful memories had resurfaced after recent events involving an important magical totem. The information they'd uncovered verified what everyone had always suspected—Carrington and Brighton Adler were murdered.

"He said he was just checking to make certain I was still watching over you." Taking a deep breath, Cooper knew this wasn't the time to dance around the phone call he'd found more than a little strange. "To be honest with you, I found the whole conversation... odd. The phone call itself wasn't particularly surprising because, at the time, you were deep undercover chasing down a data source in Indonesia." He watched a pink blush move over her cheeks, and a flash of possessiveness, unlike anything he'd ever experienced, moved through him. A growl vibrating to the surface from deep in his chest surprised them both. "We're going to table the discussion about your blush for another time."

"It isn't what you are thinking. I found a camera in my room. I didn't find the damned thing soon enough, and I've spent a lot of time and money trying to clear the internet of the pictures."

"What kind of pictures, Princess?" She'd been naked in the club more than once, and he knew, in general, shifters were pretty laisser-faire about nudity, so it seemed unlikely it was something that simple.

"The cameras were inside and outside the resort's small cabana where I stayed. I stripped inside, put on a specially made backpack before I stepped outside to shift. I'd propped the door open, so I could get inside quickly if needed. It was a short run into the woods behind the resort. My enhanced senses made it fairly simple to find what I'd been asked to retrieve. I shifted back to human form, stashed everything in my bag, then shifted again to run back to the hut. Most of the shots we've tracked down were tagged as special effects, but there seems to be just enough doubt for the damned pictures to reappear every now and again."

"Why didn't I know about this?" Was this the reason her father called him? Had Carrington Adler known their kind had been compromised? If Catalina was deemed responsible for exposing shifters to public censure, she could potentially be a target of angry peers, scientists who would study them into extinction, and traffickers looking to turn a hefty profit. Hell, the danger would come at her from every direction. Staring at him as though he'd grown a second head, Catalina finally sighed.

"I couldn't exactly recruit help from the agency, Ace. All I could do was contact Austin and let him take it over.

He's the pack Alpha, and even though we don't follow the pack hierarchy closely, there are some rules I—*now we*—have to follow. Making a choice between protecting my family and asking for help was a no-brainer, Cooper."

"Clearly, I have a lot to learn." For the first time in longer than he could remember, Cooper felt like a first-class ass. "I'm sorry, Princess. I've never been possessive of anyone other than Lakyn, never felt the overwhelming urge to protect anyone but my sister and her children. Even that loyalty and unconditional commitment pale in comparison to what I feel for you. The connection between us is growing so quickly I'm having a hard time processing the intensity of the emotions." Although he wasn't being dramatic, at times, it felt like he was drowning as the feelings crashed over him in overwhelming waves.

"The intensity of your feelings will eventually back off a bit, but they will always be stronger than those of non-shifters. The feeling your entire world has been tilted on its axis is a part of the mating process. My brothers can tell you more about it, but I don't think there is a magic potion to speed the process up." He felt his eyes widen, and for the first few seconds, he thought she was being flip with him. Tapping into her emotions, he discovered nothing but sincerity. Hell, he was starting to wonder if he would ever get used to the ways of the magic world.

"I didn't say I wanted to speed it up, which I interpret as getting over it. After waiting for you for longer than I want to admit, the last thing I want to do is rocket through our mating."

Chapter Eight

A UDRIC WALKED THROUGH the massive mahogany doors of the Magic Council's main reception room and made his way to his seat at the center of the raised horseshoe-shaped table. Early in his tenure, he'd shared the duties of chairman since the appointed positions on the magic world's governing body weren't originally set in stone. Historically, a member from each of the various groups of magicals would attend the meetings to make sure their kind were properly represented. The last century had seen many changes in the human and magical world. The Council members were now treated more like celebrity politicians than advocates for their fellow magicians. Each species of shifters held a seat, as did several groups of witches and wizards.

Calling the meeting to order, Audric didn't waste any time outlining the issue they were facing. "There is a consortium of the biggest giants in the business world planning to undermine free enterprise, so they can create a global economic system. Their purpose is entirely self-serving. This plan has been in place for many years, and for the most part, magicals have remained unaffected and, therefore, uninterested in the outcome."

"If we aren't involved, why have you called this special meeting? I'd just settled down to hibernate, Audric. It will take me the better part of a week to travel back to Alaska, and it's a long damned trek back to my den." Frederick Whitetail, a bear shifter who lived in Denali National Park, hated being teleported, so he traveled as far as possible using traditional transportation.

"You sound like a toddler who's been awakened from their nap. Somebody, find a nubby for Freddie." Ola, the oldest witch on the council, was still sharp as a tack, and her wit never seemed to age. Opal, her twin, who lived in a small town in Colorado, was even more spirited. The last time he'd spent any time with Opal, he and the spry witch drained several bottles of liquor before calling it a night.

"As you know, we have been working to find a link between several mysterious deaths in the magical community over the past few years. A good number of the ones we'd already identified were associated with the magical totem we were finally able to reassemble." The totem was now sealed safely in the depths of the Council's vault. The magic associated with the icon was stronger than any Audric had ever encountered. He'd marveled it was more powerful than King Arthur's sword, a magical object most considered nothing more than a myth by most. Excalibur was very real and sitting not far from where the reassembled totem now rested several levels below where they were assembled. That level of power was too easily corrupted, so it was stored in the only place on earth secure enough to provide the degree of protection required.

"When we lost Brighten..." Audric paused to pull in a deep, calming breath. Carrington and Brighten Adler's death had been a huge blow to the magical community but losing the immensely talented mother of ten children had been particularly difficult.

"Losing her felt like someone stole the sunshine. We all felt the loss, but it was an even bigger blow to you." Ola was right. Audric had mentored Brighten from the time she was a small child—something only a few people knew. When she died, he'd felt as though he had lost one of his own daughters. Nodding in agreement, Audric still felt the pain of losing the gifted witch—she'd been destined for so many amazing things.

"You know we have been trying to bring Catalina further into the fold—particularly after she recreated the totem without any prior knowledge of its existence or significance." Her jeweled sculpture was so close to the real thing, it had been spooky as hell. "I've spent time with Catalina recently, and I believe she possesses both her mother's incredible gifts and her father's considerable talents as well." Audric had always viewed Carrington as more magical than anyone believed—the man had simply been eclipsed by his beautiful wife.

"I don't mean to push, but I'm having trouble figuring out what the problem is. Bring her in, and let's make certain she gets the training she needs. If we don't continue training the younger generation, the dark side of our magical world will leap at the opportunity. Our apathy is the enemy's greatest strength." Once again, Audric nodded his agreement before waving his hand in the air. A series of pictures featuring Cooper Hicks played over the large screen at the other end of the room.

"I believe we have finally gained Mr. Hicks's trust. He

has agreed to help us identify the dark forces who have joined the economic consortium hellbent on turning the entire planet into their personal playground." Every generation pushed the boundaries a little bit further, but the most recent crop of political tyrants seemed to be hellbent on destroying everything that was good while promoting all the worst mankind had to offer.

"If the international consortium of bankers, royals, and unscrupulous people in political power are joining forces, we have to do something sooner rather than later." A ripple of agreement moved through the room.

"I agree. I called this meeting because I want to hear your thoughts." Audric already had a few ideas about how things should go, but at this point, he was open to suggestions. In the end, he doubted any of their plans would be worth a tinker's dam, but they needed plans in place. Dealing with the most powerful people in the world was never easy. Most of the elite class had little or no sense of empathy. Referring to them as narcissistic was laughable. In his experience, most were simply spoiled brats totally lacking in empathy.

Audric was often asked to bless new babies and generally chose to cast a spell upon the parents instead. His magic encouraged them to teach their children compassion, encouraging them to plant trees they would never sit under and to make certain their offspring understood no one owed them anything.

Four hours later, the group had agreed, protecting Catalina and her mate was second only to disbanding the economic consortium. The principle of yin and yang meant they would never be able to completely eliminate dark magic, but it needed to be brought back into balance with the good. Several of the Council members were dispatched to monitor the most powerful members of the consortium, and Freddie was already on his way back to Alaska, leaving Audric and Ola to watch Catalina.

Cameron Barnes' home was a virtual fortress. Audric enjoyed the tour he'd received from the man whose insatiable curiosity about anything magical was eclipsed only by his keen awareness of the world's rapid slide into what the two of them agreed had the potential to become exponentially worse than the Dark Ages.

Walking out of the meeting, Audric was lost in thought until Ola nudged him. Glancing over at one of his oldest and dearest friends, he was surprised to see she'd morphed into a much younger version of herself. With a quick wave of her fingers, he felt the unmistakable tingling associated with the change and knew she was now looking upon a man far younger than the elderly gent who'd been at her side a moment earlier.

"Come on, we need to let off some steam." Turning in the opposite direction of the apartments every member of the Council kept in another portion of their underground headquarters, Audric knew where the spirited woman was headed—Crystal Tavern.

One of the first things their ancestors had done after creating the Magic Council was to commission building the stronghold where they could meet safely. According to written accounts, groups of magicals carved the meeting room, then promptly built a more casual gathering spot close to a large crystal deposit. The proximity of the crystal vein woven like a white thread through the granite acted as a powerful booster for the human spirit. Crystal generated its own heat, keeping even the deepest levels of the fortress at the perfect temperature. The walls and floors themselves were warm to the touch, unlike other underground caverns.

Each member of the Council had a small apartment built along a wide corridor at the opposite side of the more commercial areas. The apartments lined both sides of a winding hallway carved in a meandering pattern, so the accommodations were close to a smaller vein of life-renewing crystal. The individual members of the governing body of magicals didn't always agree on the decisions they faced, but they all knew their small but luxurious apartments rejuvenated their spirits. Sleeping near crystal brought an increase in not only physical energy but revived mental acuity and imagination. Over the years, Audric found himself returning more often, taking advantage of the earth's unique power to recharge itself and, therefore, those who inhabited it.

"Great Goddess, you need a break, my friend. Your mind is cluttered by too much gloom and boom." Ola's teasing voice pulled him back to the moment, and he chuckled at how well she'd read him.

"You're too right. A few drinks with a dear friend is always good for the soul."

"That it is, and we're not talking shop. No business tonight."

Audric nodded in agreement. The youth spell she'd cast was temporary, and there was no reason to waste time bemoaning the problems they faced. They had solid plans in place and worrying was counterintuitive to everything the magical world believed.

Sitting on the padded leather seat, Audric slid partway around the circular booth, relishing how easily his younger body moved. Flashing Ola a quick grin, he chuckled to himself about her using her middle rather than her first name. She told him once the decision had more to do with wanting to stand out in a family where all the women were named after gemstones, and "who the hell wants to be called Iolite?" He had to admit Ola was the better alternative. Shaking his head as he watched her drain her first drink and lift the empty glass to their waiter, Audric wondered what was really behind her push for this impromptu meeting. Assured her next round was on the way, Ola turned her attention to him.

"Did I tell you Opal and Ruby are expanding the store?" Aha, perhaps this was at the heart of her discontent. He knew Ola's twin and their younger sister hoped to lure Opal's granddaughter to their Rocky Mountain hometown. The two women had been trying to get the younger witch to leave her job in Salem for some time, and he suspected expanding the store was a part of their plan.

"No, but she's a clever woman, so I'm not surprised. Perhaps the Council can help with the expansion." Ola's eyes widened, and Audric shook his head, knowing he'd given her the wrong impression. The Council didn't use magic in ways that would draw unnecessary attention, the tight-knit community Opal called home would definitely sit up and take notice if they were suddenly inundated with magical beings. "I was thinking more along the lines of advertising and promoting the store. If they expand their online presence, it could be very profitable for them. We can make certain they are able to offer the products we're currently forced to buy outside the country."

"There are too many government regulations for the things we need. I have no idea why those jackasses have such a hard-on for our goodies. I swear to the Great Goddess, it's baffling why some bureaucrat in a cheap suit and fugly tie cares about salamander eyes. The whole mess is a mystery to me."

"Fugly?"

"Yeah. Emerald said it means fucking ugly. It's my new fave word." Ola's grin was pure devilment as she waved her hand in the air, producing a bill large enough elicit an appreciative smile from the waiter. Audric didn't doubt the young wizard would keep their glasses refilled the rest of the evening.

College-aged magicals of every type could apply for positions inside the Council's headquarters. The criteria for acceptance were exceptionally strict, and Audric found himself wondering who the young waiter used as references. He'd learned long ago, knowing who an employee used as a reference often told you everything you needed to know about why they'd been hired.

"Hello?" Ola pretended to knock on his forehead, pulling Audric back to the moment. "I'm going to stop by Opal's after we set this mess back in order. I know we promised to skip talking shop, but I had a vision the other night and haven't been able to get it out of my mind." Having been married to a powerful witch for many years, Audric knew better than to discount their instincts or visions.

"We can talk about whatever we damned well please.

Tell me about the vision." Audric focused his attention on the woman sitting across from him. He'd known Ola for more years than he wanted to think about—their friendship endured despite not always sharing the same view. When his sweet Elizabeth died, Ola showed up within the hour to help him handle the arrangements. She'd been rock solid despite her own grief—Ola and Elizabeth had been close friends since childhood.

There was a point during those first dark days when he'd had to remind himself Ola was setting her own sadness aside to help him. He knew she had a reputation for being tough as nails, but the never-married witch had a heart of gold. The time she spent helping see him through those first few weeks only served to strengthen the bond between them. Audric considered Ola Stone one of his closest friends and most trusted confidants.

"What if Catalina's kidnapping was exactly what it appeared to be—an attempt to find out which agents are working both sides against the middle? Cooper comes in like an avenging angel, killing everyone standing between him and the woman he knows is his soulmate. His actions told everyone in the magic world how important Catalina was to him, but more importantly, it broadcast the same information to the Consortium." He felt his brows raise, and Ola nodded. "Yes, indeed, the very group that has been trying to recruit Cooper for the last several years."

Audric leaned back in the booth, stretching out his long legs and crossing his ankles. Sipping his drink, he let Ola's words tumble around in his mind. The information wasn't new, and if he was honest, this wasn't the first time he'd wondered if they were dealing with two different problems—distinct but overlapping.

"I admit I've considered this scenario, but knowing you've made the same observation and envisioned it, leads a lot of credence to the possibility. Catalina's magic has always been more powerful than she is aware. I still believe the kidnapping was motivated as a way to isolate her and allow the dark forces access to her."

"She attributes it to artistic whimsy or something equally bogus."

Audric didn't hold back his laughter at Ola's new slang. It was easy to see she'd been spending time with the younger magicals. He'd always thought it was unfortunate she hadn't settled down to have a family of her own since she was a natural-born mentor.

"You are terrible for a girl's ego, drifting in and out of the conversation with every little breeze. I have no idea how you are able to resist my sparkling personality and witty conversation." Audric chuckled at her teasing. Damn, it was good to have friends who weren't intimidated by his position. "If we really want to take the bastards out, all we need to do is give Lilly West a surface-to-air launcher like they had in that Arnold Schwartz movie."

Arnold Schwartz? Oh, brother. Gifted witch, but not so great with movie trivia.

"True Lies? Jamie Lee Curtis was also in that movie. Damn, that scene where she dances with the bedpost was something else. I saw an interview where she said her best work ended up on the cutting room floor because it was too suggestive." He sighed and, for the first time in over a century, wished he was younger.

"I want to meet Lilly West. I've watched her from afar.

Damn, she is a corker. I think I want to be her when I grow up." Ola's comment caught him off guard, and Audric felt his entire body convulse with laughter. The woman's sense of humor was so unexpected most of the time, he often forgot how witty she could be.

"Probably a sentiment shared by many." They spent the next hour chatting about mutual friends and speculating about which member of the Council was going to be the next to announce their retirement. There were several members who should have stepped down years ago. At this point, it was a toss-up what was the greater risk— inexperienced members or those who were literally being led around headquarters because they couldn't remember where they were headed or how to get there.

Chapter Nine

C ATALINA KICKED OFF her shoes, uncaring the rubber
soles of her cross-trainers thumped against the front
of the stackable washer and dryer. She'd been pleased to
learn the small guest house had its own laundry room—
traipsing around the Barnes home carrying dirty under-
wear hadn't sounded appealing. Still wired after spending
two hours in Cam and CeCe's enormous workout room,
Cat was practically bouncing on the balls of her feet, rolling
her eyes at the absurdity of calling it a home gym—the
spacious room was filled with so many machines it rivaled
the most upscale commercial health clubs in Austin.

"Damn it all to fucking hell. I'm going to go insane if
they don't let me go back to work. What am I supposed to
do all day? Daytime television is mind-numbing. When I
tried to clean the place, one of the maids swore at me in
Portuguese. Unfortunately for her, I understood her
accusation. Hearing her swear I'm trying to steal her job
because her boss is hung like a horse was just wrong on too
many levels. Hell, I'll probably have nightmares thinking
about how she came upon that information." Cat had been
stuck inside for days without a clue where Cooper had
gone or when he would be back. *And now I'm talking to*

myself—this disaster seems to be snowballing into a full-blown avalanche.

Catalina was struggling to come to grips with how things were playing out. The second night after they'd moved into the Barnes' guest house, Cooper's phone rang during the night. She'd been dead asleep after a scene so hot, it was nothing short of a miracle she had enough functioning brain cells to rouse at all. It wasn't until the next morning, when she awoke to an empty bed, Cat realized the ringtone had been the one Cooper assigned his handler at the agency.

She'd found a note propped in the one place he knew she wouldn't miss it—the coffeemaker. Holding the folded paper in her hand, Catalina had spent long minutes struggling to get her eyes focused on the neatly penned words. Shaking her head to clear the lingering cobwebs of sleep, Cat had sent up a quick prayer to the Great Goddess, asking her to give her an extra boost from the caffeine. When the words continued to blur across the note, Cat had only been able to sigh in frustration.

Now, several days later, she was still trying to sort it all out. Maybe she needed another cup of coffee… or two. Sitting on a tall stool at the bar, staring off into space, her unseeing gaze focused on the note she'd left on the counter. Catalina barely registered the door opening until Tobi West's voice filled the small space.

"Good morning, sunshine. How are you this morning? Oh, goody, coffee. I could use a pick me up. I overslept this morning, hell, the sun was already peeking over the horizon singing…"

"For the love of God, Tobi, give Catalina a chance to

breathe. Not everyone bounces out of bed, ready to take on the day." Gracie shook her head and rolled her eyes at her best friend and business partner before turning her attention to Cat. "Morning people just don't get it. I've never understood them How do they do it? I won't even share a hotel room with her when we travel. I live in fear I'll strangle her before I've had enough coffee to cope with her cheerful ass."

"Kent and Kyle would be pissed... probably. Well, most of the time, they wouldn't want you to strangle me. Okay, they wouldn't be happy at all, but I find it hard to believe the thought hasn't crossed their mind a time or two. Damn, it's getting late. We need to get moving if we're going to talk about what pieces we would like to have for the forum shop."

"Pieces? Like jewelry pieces?" Cat was trying desperately to keep up, but Tobi's thinking wasn't anything close to logical.

"Oh, look at you. Miss finally-turned-the-page is finally catching up. The caffeine is kicking in, isn't it?" Catalina dropped her head and sighed before turning to Gracie.

"Please make her stop. Morning people are put on Earth to torture the innocent who need a few moments for their brains to switch on." When Gracie nodded, giggling, Cat turned her attention back to the note Cooper had written.

Princess — I've gotten a solid lead on who hired the men behind the fiasco at the ceremony. Stay with Cam. He is coordinating your security with Israel. No one comes or leaves w/o his permission. Stay safe and don't forget to miss me. — Ace

"I can't believe he didn't take me. We've worked together on a lot of missions. Why would he leave me out of something this important?" She hadn't intended to speak out loud. There wasn't any reason to advertise how diminished she felt by being excluded. Damn it all to hell, he'd essentially iced her out of the entire investigation. And she wasn't even going to start on the nonsense about asking Cam Barnes' permission to leave his compound. *Yeah, that's not fucking happening.*

If you think Cam is working alone, you are sadly mistaken, sister mine. We've enlisted the help of every Dom in the club.

Israel's voice was so loud in her head, Cat almost turned to look for him. If they put her on a damned no-fly list, she was going to… hell, what could she do? Since Cooper took the call, he'd be considered the Agent in Charge and would have access to resources she didn't. Sure, she worked for the Agency occasionally, but she was considered a contractor rather than a Special Agent.

In many ways, Cat's out-of-the-box status was a blessing because it was much easier for her to walk away, unlike Cooper and Cameron. Over the years, Catalina had also worked as a special operations asset for Mossad and the Secret Intelligence Service, among others.

In Catalina's view, Americans' belief the Central Intelligence Agency was the number one intelligence organization in the world was based more on Hollywood's perception than fact. After working for each of what was considered the top ten intelligence organizations in the world, Cat held the opinion the U.S. was number three, at best. She'd met more world leaders than she could count and always marveled at how different they were from the way they were portrayed in the media.

"I don't know where she went, but it doesn't look like a happy journey." Gracie's Latina accented voice floated into the deep recesses of Cat's mind without being enough to pull her back to the present. It wasn't until she felt the paper slip from between her fingers, she realized her mind had wandered too far from the conversation. Blinking to bring the room back into focus, Cat watched Gracie and Tobi read the short note. Both women frowned but predictably, it was Tobi who found her voice first.

"He has good penmanship." Grasping her arm when Gracie slugged her with no real malice, Tobi moaned. "What? You are always screeching at me to find the silver lining in everything, so I did... and it wasn't easy because I wanted to tell Cat I think Cooper is acting like a socially inept piss pocket... but I thought that might be seen as outside the boundaries of Little Miss Sunshine and Lollipops take Austin."

"I swear to God, I don't know how you do it. I've never seen anyone talk for so long without taking a breath. It's remarkable. I'll bet your men think being able to go that long without inhaling is the best thing since sliced bread."

"If you make a blow job joke at my expense, I'm going to take you with me to pick up the pop'n fresh exploding rolls next year for the fundraiser." Gracie waved away Tobi's threat.

"That was your own fault, sister. You were born and raised in Texas. How you managed to forget how hot the interior of an enclosed car gets in the summer is a mystery for the ages."

Catalina shook her head as the two women bantered back and forth. She'd only recently heard about the exploding dough incident and wasn't surprised Tobi was still being teased.

"Boy, oh, boy, do you think anybody is ever going to cut me a break on that mess? Hell, no. Those jackasses running the wrecker took enough pictures to feed the internet for the next hundred years. Even my kids still laugh about me killing the Pillsbury Dough Boy. It's ridiculous. I didn't kill the giggling, sticky little creep. I set him free. He should be grateful."

Catalina couldn't hold back her laughter, and Gracie rolling her dark eyes with enough drama to earn an Oscar nomination was like throwing gas on a fire. Cat fell into a fit of giggles that was likely as much from the emotional roller coaster she'd been riding for the past several weeks as the women who'd done a bang-up job of distracting her.

Once she'd finally recovered enough to excuse herself, Cat was surprised to find the closet filled with her clothes. Dressing casually, she brushed her hair, dabbed on some mascara, then headed back to the small living room. Coming to a dead stop, Cat stared at the boxes sitting on every available flat surface. Looking at Tobi and Gracie, she cocked her brow and waited for them to explain.

"Hey, girl, don't be giving us that look. This is all on the Doms. We didn't have anything to do with this."

"Well, that isn't entirely true, Tobi." Turning back to Cat, Gracie explained, "We asked if we could take you into town to visit your store. We wanted to check out your line of kinky jewelry." Shrugging the lovely Latina, added,

"You'd have thought we asked to help you escape from some high-security prison. I swear the President travels with less planning."

"Oh, yeah, I nearly fell asleep listening to the logistics lecture." Tobi rolled her eyes so far, Cat would bet her friend had seen the inside of her own head. "I swear I have that speech memorized. They really need to rewrite the script."

"An unnecessary drain on resources better utilized to finding those responsible."

"Not reasonable to take the unwarranted risks."

"We have an obligation to her Dom to keep her in the safest possible environment." Gracie hadn't missed a beat in their back and forth outlining of the lecture they'd both received. "We didn't know they were going to do this, but we'll roll with it since they just texted to say they are having lunch and drinks catered by the pool."

It didn't take long to unpack the boxes. Whoever put the jewelry trays inside had been meticulous with the packing—only one tray per box with enough cushioning to ensure nothing moved around on the velvet display boards. The care in packaging spoke volumes. There was no question—her sister Asia had overseen this process. No one else had Asia's eye for perfection. Catalina didn't think she'd ever appreciated her big sister's obsessive-compulsive organizational skills more.

Sitting back, sipping the smoothie Cam and CeCe's personal chef had delivered, Cat closed her eyes and groaned. The man was clearly a magician with food. If there was ever a reason to stay put, it would be Henry's kitchen skills.

"Cam knows just how to ensnare the fly in his trap." Tobi's voice was comically sinister, pulling Catalina out of her delicious distraction. "The sugar rush fuels a sense of well-being."

"Followed by the crash, which leaves the prisoner too lethargic to consider moving, let alone making a sincere effort to escape."

Gracie's ability to tag-team with Tobi's off the wall sense of humor might have been more impressive if Catalina hadn't recognized their understated warning. Cat noted the way Gracie's eyes flickered up and to the left, but Catalina was too well-trained to immediately follow the other woman's gaze. Hell, as a skilled operative, Catalina didn't need to look. She'd spotted the nearly hidden cameras within seconds of her arrival yesterday, but she appreciated Gracie's subtle reminder.

Working with Tobi and Gracie was a cross between hysterical and baffling. Catalina knew the two women built their business from the ground up and had recently taken it international. They weren't traveling much anymore, proving it was possible to continue growing a successful business via technology. Gracie and Tobi both swore while they enjoyed meeting club owners face to face, they didn't miss airport security.

"Tobi is a damned trouble magnet. I swear there could be a hundred people in line, and they will pull her out for a pat-down every flippin' time. I don't know if it's those long blonde waves, her curves, or her mouth that attracts attention."

"Hey, what the holy Hannah is that supposed to mean? I'm not mouthy. I could have filed sexual assault charges against that jackass in Newark."

"You'd be sunning yourself in Club Fed if it wasn't for Ian." Gracie hadn't missed a beat, even though she'd appeared engrossed in the close examination of a clit clip set. "This set is exquisite. I love the sapphire insets. We could also do special orders."

"Yes, Doms would love to pick the stones for their sub. Birthstones, rocks to match their collar or eyes, something to remind them of the Caribbean Sea. For a bunch of whip-wielding bossy-boots, they can be really romantic."

Catalina felt her mouth drop open. *Whip wielding bossy-boots?* Gracie must have seen Cat's quick glance toward the poorly concealed camera. The grin spreading over her face was a dead giveaway, they'd be hearing more about Tobi's comment… and if Cat's guess was right, the two women were looking forward to it.

"Tobi, you know Cam is going to throw you under the bus so fast, you aren't going to have time to explain to Kent and Kyle. All we're going to hear is the thump, thump of tires running you over."

"Posh." Tobi interrupted her friend and waved her hand, clearly dismissing her concern. "Do you know how many people throw my happy ass under the bus on a daily basis? The number is mind-boggling. One look from Kyle and everybody and their damned dog turns into a blasted snitch. Then we have the Spies-R-Us wannabes with their damned cell phones. Remember when that heathen bitch almost ran over me last month?" Turning to Catalina, Tobi explained.

"I had a flat tire on the highway a couple of miles from home. I know how to change tires, but my husbands get all grinchy when I do it, so I was standing off the side of the road. I must have been a solid ten to fifteen feet off the road, and this lunatic newbie sub from the club comes racing by. Crazy girl is so busy checking out my car and dialing her damned phone, she went off the road and almost hit me. What the hell? I was still so mad when Kent got there, I was raving like a lunatic." By this time, Tobi's arms were flailing in the air as she stormed around the small room like a tiny blonde tornado.

"You know who Ditzy Dolly was calling? Prairie Winds. She told Kent I wasn't anywhere to be seen. Good grief, try looking out your damned windshield instead of at your phone, Nutso Nelly. After learning what happened, Kent wanted to call her Dom, but I asked him to talk to her himself. I know what it's like being tattled on, and it sucks. Hell, at this point, my men would be more worried if someone wasn't tossing me in front of a speeding Greyhound."

"I don't understand. If she recognized your car, why didn't she stop and check on you herself?" Catalina was always shocked when women didn't help one another. She and her sisters learned early in life how important it was to empower each other.

"She has a lot to learn, and there are some painful lessons in her future at the club. Tobi didn't share the story with the other subs, but... what did you call her? Ditzy Dolly? Oh, yeah, she's earned her nickname. The woman actually told some of the other subs at the club what she'd done... including Jen McCall." Catalina had only met Jen a few times, but she'd been drawn to her take no prisoners attitude.

"I can tell by the look on your face you know how well that went over. Jen let her have it with both barrels. The entire locker room was filled with Doms and subs by the time it was all done." Tobi's eyes were practically dancing with glee. "And the best part? Sam and Sage led the applause when Jen was done." Tobi's excitement was more subdued now, a sheen of tears, making her eyes appear glassy. "I hope the woman learns a lesson from this mess. First, she damned well shouldn't be on her phone while driving by a disabled vehicle."

"She should stop and help when she recognizes the vehicle. Might be nice if she'd think about something other than making herself look important to the owners of the club." Gracie's observation was likely dead on.

Catalina was still reeling. She hadn't lived in Austin full time for several years, and it was sad to think her hometown had lost some of its small-town charm and friendliness.

"Let's move this outside. I'm anxious to find out what's for lunch. I bet it's spectacular. Grab a notebook, and let's talk orders and prices." Tobi gave Catalina a cat that swallowed the canary grin, "Hope you're ready for what's headed your way. You're going to need to hire help... probably a lot of help. Maybe a magic wand would help." Tobi burst out laughing at her own joke as they headed outside.

"She doesn't need a wand to do magic, and there won't be a need for hocus pocus since she's partnering with Ian McGregor. I swear his organization is the most efficiently run corporation on the planet. He should run for president." By the time they settled down with their plates of food, they'd named a dozen reasons the entrepreneur and Dom would never consider politics. In Catalina's opinion, all the reasons centered around one theme—Ian was simply too honest.

Chapter Ten

C OOPER MOVED EASILY through the security checkpoint at JFK International. There were definitely perks to working for the Agency. Striding down the long hallway to his assigned gate, the hair on the back of his neck started to stand on end. Cooper had been an agent too long to ignore the warning.

Stepping into a deserted alcove, he took a deep breath and tuned into his surroundings. Not sensing any immediate danger, he redirected his energy to retrace everything that had transpired over the past few hours. So much had happened over the previous two years, Cooper was worried he hadn't taken time to piece everything together. As seemingly unrelated facts moved through his mind, he felt Israel's unmistakable mental connection.

Twenty minutes after your flight left Austin, someone tried to break into Adler Oil. The son of a bitch got away, but he dropped the small satchel he was carrying. Cooper heard a huge unspoken but, so he waited for Israel to finish. Telepathic communication was unnerving, but it was also damned handy. *The asshat had a copy of your preliminary blueprints for the remodel.* It took every ounce of control he possessed to withhold the string of curses simmering in his gut like a cauldron of poison. *Who knew you were leaving?*

Before Cooper could answer, his phone rang. The unique ringtone he'd assigned his handler at the Agency saved him looking at the screen.

"Hicks." Cooper didn't feel any obligation to be polite to the man he'd only been working with a few years. He'd never been able to establish any rapport or trust with Damon Garrison. There was something about the man that made him uneasy.

Trust your instincts—always.

Knowing Israel was still plugged into his thoughts was oddly comforting.

"Your contact in Berlin is the same one who cleared Catalina to enter Landstuhl Regional Medical Center." Cooper felt his blood run cold as realization washed over him. No one at the Agency knew who'd helped him get Cat into the largest military hospital outside the U.S. Cameron Barnes had been his liaison stateside, but even Cam didn't know who'd facilitated Catalina's admission into the base and medical center.

Don't get on the plane, Cooper. It's a fucking set up. I'm calling Ian now. Don't leave the airport. Buy a disposable phone and call me. It will take us a half hour to tag your sat phone and make it look like you're on the plane.

"Hicks? What the fuck? Are you listening to me?" Garrison's irritation fueled Cooper's concern. If the man didn't have a personal stake in the mission, there would be no reason for his impatience.

"It's rude to speak on the phone while you're ordering food, Garrison. I will contact him as soon as I land. Thanks for the heads up; text me the rest. My food is ready."

Disconnecting the call without giving the other man a chance to reply might have been rude, but Cooper's control was slipping. The sudden realization the man who was entrusted with his safety was compromised was damned scary. Piecing together the snippets that hadn't made any sense was much easier now. Damon Garrison had just signed his life away. Endangering Catalina in his effort to frame Cam and Cooper for whatever the pissant was into was all the motivation Hicks needed to take him out.

Ten minutes later, Cooper walked out of the airport's phone store. The clerk activated the phone, and Cooper couldn't hold back his bark of laughter when the damned thing rang five minutes later.

"You'll only be able to use that phone until you meet my staff outside baggage claim." Cooper might not have been able to identify the number, but Ian McGregor's velvet-smooth voice was easy to recognize. There were very few men in the world with the resources to tag a phone within minutes, and Ian was at the top of the list. "Smith will be standing twenty yards to the right of the door leading to the street. He's almost seven feet tall, so he'll be easy to spot."

"I'll be there in five minutes. I need to get back to Texas."

"I'll have a jet waiting for you at a private airport outside Newark. Everything about the flight plan is bogus, so don't be surprised when the crew clears for Kansas City. There's a hell of a storm moving into that area, so you'll be diverted to Austin." McGregor's ability to pull a plan together out of thin air never ceased to amaze him. Cooper was grateful for the man's help and told him so. "You know I have a vested interest, Cooper. I'm looking forward to having you available for security consultations, and I care very much about keeping Catalina safe as well. She is more than a business partner, she's a friend."

Cooper didn't get a chance to respond before Ian ended the call. Shaking his head, Cooper stepped out of the baggage claim area and walked toward the giant leaning against the wall. With any luck, he'd be back in Austin before Catalina woke up. Keeping her in bed all day would be a great way to expend the energy he could feel roiling in his gut.

Following Ian's man to the car, Israel's voice sounded loud and clear in Cooper's mind.

Luke is all over Garrison like a bad rash. What he can't find, he'll probably plant. For a nerd, he's a formidable enemy.

Garrison didn't get the job of handler by being smart. He's somebody's butt plug nephew's third cousin twice removed.

Good to know, that should make Luke's work easier and cross one felony off the list.

Cooper caught himself before he laughed out loud. No need to tell everyone around him he was hearing voices. They'd probably alert the authorities, thinking he'd lost his mind. The last place he wanted to be was some damn psych ward, waiting on an evaluation. He'd helped send more than one enemy into those hellholes and had no desire to join them.

LEANING BACK AGAINST the sun-warmed fabric of her

lounger, Tobi lifted her glass of iced tea. Rubbing the cool glass over her face, she took a deep breath and giggled.

"Gracie, tell Catalina about the cookbooks we invested in." When she heard Cat gasp in surprise, Tobi sighed. "Damn, I was hoping you hadn't already heard about my culinary challenges."

"Tobi, there isn't a soul in Austin who hasn't been regaled with at least one tale of your cooking disasters." Gracie turned to look at Tobi, pushing her blinged-out sunglasses down her upturned nose and shaking her head at her friend. "I'm not saying my culinary expertise is anything to write home about, but at least I'm not banned from the kitchen."

"Banned?" Catalina was surprised, despite having heard more than one story about Tobi's cooking disasters. "Who on earth would ban you from your own kitchen?"

"Oh, I'm not banned from entering, but the staff won't let me near any appliance that generates heat or spins. I'm going to talk to Ian about inventing a stove that shuts itself off before the smoke detector gets involved... and a blender that won't start until the lid is secured."

"Cooper's sister, Lakyn, is an author. She would love these stories."

Gracie burst out laughing at Cat's comment as Tobi visibly flinched.

"She has interviewed Tobi several times. Have you heard Ian talk about his friends in Colorado?"

"He has mentioned Alex and Zach Lamont a couple of times, but it was always related to security issues." Cat wasn't sure how the Lamonts fit into this conversation, but she'd learned conversations with Tobi and Gracie didn't always flow in a linear direction. Before the dynamic duo could explain, the sound of approaching footsteps had Cat sitting up. Her enhanced hearing was a huge advantage on missions. Aside from that, it was often annoyingly distracting when she was working. The soft sound of the footfalls belonged to someone accustomed to moving stealthily—Cam.

Cam Barnes wasn't given to social calls and certainly wouldn't voluntarily drop in on three women drinking and lounging around his pool in the middle of the day unless his wife was involved. Not that he was above keeping an eye on them, but that was what surveillance equipment was for. Whatever prompted him to disturb the women must be important.

Nodding to Tobi and Gracie, Cam gave them a smile that didn't reach his eyes. "Ladies, there is a car waiting out front to take you back to Prairie Winds. Thank you for visiting my guest. Make sure you let her know what pieces you are interested in and a timeline." They all three stared at him for long seconds trying to wrap their minds around this strange foray into their business dealings. "I've already told your men you are heading home, so it probably isn't wise to delay."

"Well, if that doesn't beat all. Invite us over and then kick us to the curb." Tobi stood from her chair, hands on her hips, glaring at Cam, though he was clearly unfazed.

"Cameron, I must say, your hospitality skills need polishing." Gracie might have taken a swipe at their host, but she wasn't wasting any time gathering her things and heading for the door.

"We'll be in touch, Catalina. We really are fully committed to working with you. We'll email our list and plan to meet again after we get a date set for a special event showing." Stopping in front of Catalina, the petite blonde's eyes were filled with something between concern and annoyance. Casting a glance to where Cam stood nearby, Tobi's lips pressed together in a firm line. "If you need us, call. We'll help in any way we can… and we can be pretty creative."

Cam's soft chuckle let them know Tobi's unspoken message hadn't been wasted. Waiting until she heard the door close after Tobi left was an exercise in patience, Cat turned to Cam the second she knew they were alone.

"Talk to me, Cam. Is Cooper okay?"

"Cooper is fine, but there have been some complications. I'm worried you are no longer safe here."

"You know who's on the inside, don't you? You've figured out who is trying to frame the two of you?" Catalina had never been particularly empathic, but Cam was practically radiating with anger he was trying to hide. "Holy hell, which handler? His point man at the Agency called during the night, so I'm guessing it's Cooper's. He has to be setting up the two of you for something, but what?" Cam's lack of response spoke volumes.

"I've had a bag packed for you." Before he could continue, Cat interrupted.

"Where is your family?" She was terrified they'd brought trouble to Cam's doorstep.

"Cecelia is at the hospital and safe. I'll pick her up myself after I take you to the airport."

Cat wasn't surprised she was being moved, but she hoped they weren't sending her anywhere cold. A beach with fruity drinks with little umbrellas would be perfect... which meant they would probably send her to fucking Alaska.

Close. For somebody who traveled all over the world, you sure are a lightweight.

Leave it to Israel to be tapped in when she least expected it. Instead of asking where she was headed, Cat waited.

"The kids are at Kent and Kyle's. They'll be safe there, and they're having a great time. I suspect they are plotting ways to take over the world." His half-smile was filled with affection. Cameron Barnes would never be fully free from his former life as an operative, but his devotion to his family pushed him to continue taking whatever steps necessary to keep them safe. "Sage and Sam are escorting you to ShadowDance. Jen is tagging along, so you don't get steamrolled by the testosterone tanks—her words, not mine."

"I'll appreciate her company. I'd like to grab a few things you might have forgotten. It'll take me only a minute." Dashing inside, Cat grabbed a sketch pad and several small weapons she'd hidden in the cottage. Not only would they come in handy, but she also didn't want anyone else stumbling upon them. The great thing about flying private was the ease of traveling with the weapons she needed to feel safe.

Chapter Eleven

C ATALINA LAUGHED WHEN Jen scrambled into the co-pilot's seat as Sage began their descent into the small airport. Chattering a mile a minute about how much fun it was to slide between mountain peaks, anticipating the shifting air currents, her words were quickly lost in the changing roar of the jet. Nothing Jen mentioned sounded like fun to Cat, but it didn't matter how many times she flew, there was always a part of her that worried the damned plane was going to fall out of the air.

"Remember, my lovely wife is not the one at the controls. She likes to watch Sage work." Sam's quiet reassurance was appreciated, even if it was humbling.

"I wasn't worried... not really." She sighed and tried to relax back into her seat. "I guess I should stop thinking about everything that could go wrong and concentrate on what's gone right."

"I agree, in theory, but you know as well as I do, that doesn't work out well for operatives. Planning for every contingency is how we stay alive." He was right, and it surprised her how quickly she'd stopped considering herself a member of the intelligence community. Shifting to full-time jewelry design was easier than she'd anticipated—or at least it would be if she and Cooper could stop dodging the daggers being hurled their way.

"We'll be on the ground in five minutes. It's a steep drop, so make sure everything is secured." Sage's voice came over the speakers, his tone all business, a big change from the way he'd been chatting through the open doorway a few minutes earlier. Sage appeared to be the more amiable of the two McCall brothers, but Catalina suspected they were equally dominant when it came to their free-spirited wife. Jen, a former State Department employee who spoke several languages, walked away from her career after being held hostage in a South American embassy. According to Cooper, Jen had taken to mission operations like a duck to water.

While Sam closed the laptop he'd been working on and slid it back into the largest backpack she'd ever seen, Cat fastened her seatbelt. Turning her attention to the mountains outside her window, she cringed when she saw snow capping the peaks. The fall colors were beautiful, but Catalina knew the weather in the Rockies was fickle.

I have to be the only shifter on the planet who hates cold weather.

True to his word, Sage touched down within minutes. Making her way carefully down the jet's steep steps to what turned out to be a remarkably short blacktop runway, Cat sagged with relief to see Cooper leaning casually against a large black SUV. Her heart skipped a beat before pounding erratically when his scent caught the wind. For several seconds, she stood rooted in place, unable to move as a wave of lust crashed over her.

"Damn, girl. Your man looks like he wants to eat you

alive. What are you standing here for? Go get him."

Jen's not so gentle nudge sent Cat stumbling forward, but it was the push she'd needed. Sprinting the short distance, Cat wanted to laugh when his eyes widened at her speed. Cooper barely had time to shift positions before she leaped into his arms.

"Princess, you never fail to surprise me." He hugged her tightly against his chest, his chuckle vibrating all the way to her core. Cat couldn't wait to get to wherever they were staying. She wanted him naked and inside her—now would be better, but soon would have to do. Catalina felt his entire body stiffen as a growl broke free, his warm breath moving over the shell of her ear.

"Hold that thought, mate." Setting her on her feet, Cooper walked her around to the passenger side, settling her on the heated leather seat. "Wait here while I get your luggage. When I come back, I want your jeans and panties around your ankles. Make sure your legs are spread wide enough I can see what's mine."

The words sent a rush of cream to her sex. Thank Goddess, she'd noted the towel folded on the center console. Moving the seat back as far as it would go, Cat tried to keep her movements subtle in hopes the trio chatting with Cooper wouldn't notice. The penetrating look in Sam's gaze and sly grin curving Sage's lips assured her the effort had been wasted. Catalina finally settled into position, grateful the heated seat warmed the towel quickly. Making eye contact with Jen, the other woman gave her a quick thumbs-up before turning back to the jet and making her way up the steps, followed by her husbands. Cooper jogged back to the SUV, loaded her bags in the back, then settled in the driver's seat. Pulling her close, he pressed his lips to hers for a quick kiss.

"I can't tell you how much I want to fuck you. Right here. Right now." The words were whispered against her trembling lips. Need swamped her, pulsing so deep in her pussy, the sensation sent a wash of slick cream to her opening. When he finally put a few inches between them, Cat watched Cooper's nostrils flare. "Your scent makes me so hard, I can barely think. Hell, half my blood is rocketing to my cock—it'll be a damned miracle if I can drive." His gaze dropped to her bare thighs, his fingers trailing up the sensitive inside on their way to her soaked sex. "Lean your seat back a little more." She complied, hoping he'd slip his fingers into her folds. *Damn, this mating business isn't for pussies.* The thought moved through her mind, and a second later, she heard Cooper's soft laugh against her ear. "Princess, the only pussy I am interested in is the pretty pink folds displayed so perfectly between your slender thighs."

Putting the vehicle in gear, he drove quickly away from the jet already taxing down the short blacktop runway. Turning onto a narrow tree-lined road, Cooper slowed and slipped his hand between her legs. This time there were no preliminaries—the calloused pad of his finger circled her clit twice, making her arch into his touch.

"Let me know how it feels, Princess. I want to hear all those sweet moans and gasps of pleasure as you let yourself fall into the pleasure." His voice was rapidly becoming roughened by desire, the commands harsher—more demanding. Catalina wouldn't have been able to remain silent if she'd tried. They hadn't been apart long, but early in the mating process, even a few hours could be excruciating.

Letting herself express pleasure during any sexual interlude had been impossible until Cooper. She might have avoided him when they first met, but she'd always known they were fated mates. She'd lost interest in dating other men after they met, despite what she'd led him to believe.

His fingers were pure magic—stroking the slick petals of her labia, circling her clit, and pushing deep enough to make her wish she could climb onto his lap.

"Too much thinking and not enough talking, Cat. If I have to pull the car off the road, we're going to give anyone nearby a show they won't soon forget." A resounding *yes* was her first and only thought before their minds connected, and she saw the scene he was envisioning.

Seeing herself leaning over the sloped hood of the SUV, her ass bared to anyone who happened by while he alternately spanked and fucked her was a hot scene, but not the way she wanted to be introduced to the neighborhood. She'd done some quick research during the flight and discovered the Lamont family was one of the largest landowners in the area. There was no reason to give the prestigious family a reason to send her back to Texas in shame.

"Princess, I dare you to figure out a way to embarrass Alex and Zach Lamont. And I can assure you public sex would be one of the last things you'd find effective. Getting one up on them would be like trying to sexually intimidate Kent or Kyle West. What do you think you'd need to do... how extreme would the measure need be to make Ian McGregor blush?"

All the time he'd been speaking, Cooper's fingers played her like a finely tuned musical instrument. Cat could feel her breathing becoming more erratic and knew her heart rate was accelerating. The flush of arousal was moving over her chest like someone was pouring molten lava into her veins.

"Did I tell you about the last time I visited Ian and Callie's home? Walking into his office, the first thing I see is Callie standing in the corner with her dress pulled up around her waist, her blistered bottom bared for all to see. Princess, there were already three other men in the room awaiting my arrival. They were having a casual conversation about something inane while Ian's lovely sub stood silently a few feet away."

Catalina wasn't completely surprised. She knew Ian and Callie were completely immersed in the lifestyle. She'd visited Club Isola on several occasions and knew the couple's scenes were highly anticipated for a reason. Watching Ian with a single-tail whip was as frightening as it was erotic as he laid perfectly spaced stipes diagonally down Callie's slender back. By the time the last lash fell, Ian had needed only to command her release, and his lovely wife had come so hard, the bindings securing her to the St. Andrew's cross were the only things keeping her from melting into the floor.

THE WOMAN WAS going to drive him insane. He'd started talking about Ian and Callie, hoping to distract himself from the wet, velvet heat surrounding his fingers. She'd taken up where he'd left off, filling in with mental pictures of a scene she'd watched between the McGregor's that was so hot, he'd worried his cock was going to burst. Hell, everything Catalina Adler did ramped up his desire to claim her as his in every way possible.

Cooper wanted to make Catalina's every dream come true. He wanted to help her build a business she could be proud of, no matter how commercially successful it was. He hoped she would accept the Magic Council's guidance because he believed a position on the respected governing body was in her future. Most of all, Cooper wanted to see her smile, to know she was happy and fulfilled. One of the things he appreciated the most about her family was the way they supported one another. The Adlers always had one another's back.

Watching his sister's husbands, seeing how protective they were as they encouraged her to take professional and personal risks, she never would have considered without their support, was another lesson he'd learned well. The past few years had shown him how deep and all-encompassing love could be—it had been life-changing.

"You're so wet for me, Princess. It's a fucking turn-on to know you want me as much as I want you." The muscles lining her vaginal walls pulsed around his fingers, rippling as they tried to pull him deeper. Cooper had been a sexual Dominant since his teens, yet never had a woman respond to him the way Catalina did. Brilliant. Talented, Hotter than hell. *And mine!*

"Please." Her soft plea was music to his ears. Cooper could hardly wait to feel her release wash over his fingers. Pulling off the road, he parked between two large evergreens. The spot wouldn't offer much in the way of privacy, but he knew they weren't going to be here long—Cat was too close. He wanted to give her the release her body was racing toward, and he wanted to watch.

"Look at me, Catalina. I want to watch your eyes turn amber when you come for me. Seeing the change as you lose yourself in the pleasure only I can give you is fucking hot, and I damned sure wasn't going to miss it by driving." The electricity generated between the two of them was so intense, blue sparks snapped in the air. Laughing to himself, he admitted it wasn't the fireworks he was going for, but it would have to be good enough until they were both naked. *No bed required.*

Chapter Twelve

"WHERE IS OUR lovely wife?" Zach's teasing grin threatened to grate on Alex's last nerve.

"She was supposed to be checking on Jenna and Colt's old suite." 'Suite' was an understatement of mammoth proportions. Their sister and brother-in-law occupied one wing of the enormous U-shaped property. The two were currently traveling abroad, enjoying a much-needed vacation after several years of college classes for Jenna as she transitioned careers. Care of their children had fallen largely on Colt's shoulders, and despite all the added responsibility, he'd never let his duties at ShadowDance suffer.

Alex was thrilled the couple finally accepted Daniel and Catherine Lamont's offer to keep the kids while they spent some quality time together. As far as Alex was concerned, the only problem was his, Zach, and Katarina's kids also wanted to stay in town with their grandparents. He hadn't wanted to subject their parents to what he was convinced would be hell on earth, but at this point, he didn't have any other option. He and his brother had been in trouble more often than not, but their kids were next level.

"I checked it an hour ago—it was perfect. What could

she possibly be doing?" Alex understood his brother's frustration. If they didn't watch Katarina closely, she micromanaged things into oblivion... and herself into exhaustion. "Two minutes. That's all I'm going to give her, then I start a search and rescue mission that will end with her bare ass over my knee." Alex chuckled to himself. Everyone always assumed he was the stricter Dom, but Zach was easily his equal. When people saw Zach's easy smile and casual manner as weakness, they'd already been played.

Watching his twin stare at his watch, Alex rolled his eyes. "You're really going to count it down? Why don't you call her?"

"I tried." Zach pulled Katarina's pink phone from his pocket. "She's getting swats for this as well." Alex leaned back in his leather office chair and grinned. Their lovely wife should be glad their kids had been allowed a weekend in town with their grandparents and cousins. They were always careful to keep the more intimate details of their D/s relationship private and away from the prying eyes of their children. Their daughter, Mary Catherine, in particular, was far too astute and a damned snoop of the first order.

Sliding the phone across the desk, Zach nodded to the door a split second before Katarina burst in. He and his brother were both so attuned to their woman, they usually knew within a few seconds when she was going to show up.

"Have you seen my phone? I swear I had it with me until... ummm." They watched as her eyes landed on the sparkling pink rhinestone case. "Oh. Well, maybe it's been missing a little longer than I thought. You know how it is when I'm busy... time gets away from me. I was checking to make sure everything is ready for our guests' arrival. I'm anxious to meet Catalina. Tobi has told me so much about her and the cool kinky jewelry she makes. They are already working on sending some samples up for you to display in the club. It sounds like she is working with Ian, so that should speed up the manufacturing process, or maybe he's just involved in the spyware pieces? Who knows? Have you talked to Ian? I hope you aren't going to clamp monitoring equipment to my pink bits."

Alex listened to their wife chatter nervously as she inched her way closer to the phone mere inches from his fingertips. He planned to give her the chance to come clean about how long she'd been without the device she was supposed to carry at all times, but it didn't seem like that was going to happen.

Glancing at Zach, Alex saw amusement lighting his eyes. As mirror-image twins, they not only looked identical, but their thoughts were also almost always in synch as well. When she made a grab for the gaudy device, he clamped his hand around her wrist. Her startled yelp of surprise was followed by a deep flush staining her cheeks.

"Not so fast, my love." Pulling her around the desk until she stood between his spread knees, he bit back a smile at the shudder he felt move through her. It would always be a verbal sparring match with their spirited woman—it was vital to keep a tight rein on their lovely sub. If they didn't stay several steps ahead, she'd lead them around by their noses Using her free hand, Kat twirled a long blonde curl around her finger, batting her blue eyes at him with feigned innocence that was a phony as a three-dollar bill.

"I'm sure it was on my desk earlier. I was in a rush to make sure things were perfect… you know, flowers in the entry and hall tables, more sophisticated arrangements on the dining room table, and…"

"Kitten, we don't give a rat's ass about the flowers, and I can assure you, Cooper Hicks won't give two shits either. He is bringing Catalina here to keep her safe. They know this isn't a five-star resort and won't be expecting you to treat them like royalty. Now, stop trying to blow smoke up our asses. I've had your phone in my pocket for over two hours. It was left upstairs in your closet."

Alex chuckled to himself, watching what was essentially foreplay. No wonder she hadn't been able to find it. The room next to their bedroom had once been a nursery suite. Once their kids moved to their own rooms, they'd converted the rooms into a retreat for their wife—including what he was convinced had to be the largest closet west of the Mississippi River.

Without missing a beat, Kat plundered on as if Zach had never spoken. "Did I tell you everything is in place for dinner?" Once a week, they hosted an exclusive dinner party for like-minded couples. Their clear glass dining room table was perfect for everyone's viewing pleasure. Submissives were either naked or scantily clad, which always made things interesting. Yes, indeed, the views were spectacular. "Do you think Cooper and Catalina will be here in time to join us? Did you warn them about how it works? Who's planning to attend? With Jenna and Colt out of town, there's room for our guests. Have you already invited people?"

If Alex hadn't been annoyed with her, he'd have taken time to enjoy his sub's obvious discomfort. He wasn't above playing a game of cat and mouse when he knew it would end up with her over his lap—unfortunately, they didn't have enough time to entertain such nonsense. Zach should be the one to punish her, but they'd vowed to never do so while angry, so it would be his responsibility this time. Alex wondered how men who didn't have poly-amorous relationships handled amazing women like the one fidgeting nervously in front of him. It was difficult for the two of them to keep up with their wife—just the thought of doing it alone was far too humbling.

Slipping his hand into the center drawer of his desk, Alex grabbed the thick wood ruler he kept for her punish-ments. When her eyes landed on the eighteen-inch flexible metal one he used for work, he saw her stiffen. Kat's breathing ratcheted up until it was fast and much too shallow—beneath his fingers, her pulse rate spiked. Damn it, she hadn't had a panic attack in several years. Closing the drawer, Alex pulled her onto his lap. Zach was beside them by the time Alex got her settled.

"Breathe, kitten. Come on, follow my lead. In." It took Zach several seconds to gain her attention, but when she finally looked up, Alex knew she was going to be fine. "That's it. Nice and easy.'

"We promised we'd never use that on you again, love. We all learned a valuable lesson that night." Had they ever. He and Zach wanted to push her boundaries, and despite their repeated reminders for her to use her safeword if she needed to, the scene had gone way too far. The flashback

Katarina experienced that night had been heartbreaking to watch. The guilt they felt when they'd left bruises so severe, she'd barely been able to sit for weeks had gutted them both. Alex and Zach had wanted to push her but made the colossal mistake of letting their emotions over-rule their training. He and Zach both missed the signs of her distress, attributing the responses to being over-whelmed by arousal.

"I'm sorry." Kat's whispered words brought him back to the moment, and the shimmering tracks of her tears threatened to tear his heart right out of his chest. This wasn't the time to punish her for leaving her phone. They had more important things to attend to and making certain their wife understood she was theirs to love and protect was at the top of the list.

"WHAT'S THE RULE about your cell phone, love?" Alex's voice had been too calm for her comfort. Either he was distracted by the fact they had guests arriving in the next hour, or he was trying to keep Zach from blowing a gasket... which from his steamed expression was a distinct possibility. Damn, she hated that blasted phone. When had what was supposed to be a device designed for her conven-ience become a damned anchor? She'd grown tired of the tacky phone cover, too, but refused to give it up out of sheer stubbornness.

It was no secret both her husbands hated the pink case her children picked out when they were in kindergarten. She'd kept it longer than she should have because she could still remember the looks on their little faces as she'd ooh'd and ahh'd when she'd first opened their special gift. Alex's hand tightened around her wrist, bringing her back to the moment. Not only was she babbling, now she'd zoned out, too. *Damn, damn, and double damn.*

"Do you need help focusing, Katarina?" Uh oh. She knew those words were code for paddling her bare backside until she lost her damned mind—not that she was opposed to erotic spankings that ended in mind-blowing organisms. No, she was all about happy endings, but he was entirely too calm, and Zach still looked like his head was going to spin around on his shoulders with steam billowing from his ears.

Seeing the wicked metal ruler in Alex's desk sent her ass-over-teakettle into a full-blown panic attack. Her mind blanked. All she could remember was the searing pain she'd endured at the hands of a madman in a California BDSM club. Two bad scenes in her entire life, and now it seemed the memories were overlapping—not good. *Overprotection mode engaging in three... two... one.*

Kat's mind felt like it had suddenly been moved outside her body. Her head was spinning as black dots danced in front of her eyes. Zach's voice broke through the encroaching fog, but it took several long seconds for her body to respond to his command to breathe. Moving her focus to something as simple as inhaling and exhaling helped, but she'd learned a long time ago it was the restoration of oxygen to her brain that made all the difference.

Just your luck, girl. The only functional part of your psyche is the internal voice no one else can hear.

Chapter Thirteen

CATALINA WAS GRATEFUL for the Lamonts' hospitality. Their home was amazing, and Katarina was gracious as they were shown where they'd be staying, but she'd seemed oddly restrained. Alex and Zach hovered, and Catalina caught several sideways glances, almost as though they felt their pretty wife was too fragile to be left without one of them at her side. The odd feeling they'd walked into the middle of... something unusual was so distracting, she'd almost missed Alex's comments about dinner.

Holy shit, did he just say they hosted a kink meal once a week?

She felt Cooper's arms encircle her from behind, pulling her back against his chest and rapidly inflating cock.

"What do you think, Princess? Are you up to playing at dinner? Or are you too tired?" Damn him. He knew exactly how to throw down the challenge. To anyone who didn't know her, it might seem as though he'd given her an opportunity to bow out gracefully, but she knew better.

"I'd like to be seated near Katarina. I've seen some of her web-design work, and I'd like to get a head-start persuading her to set up something for me. Ian suggested I try to get her on our team sooner rather than later."

So there. Take that, my railroading mate. She felt him chuckling behind her and smiled to herself when she heard his barely audible, "Touché."

"It should be interesting. There are other couples attending, and I'm anxious to see how confusing it gets with your names being so similar." Zach's parting comment made her smile.

She didn't have any doubt the dinner would be interesting and wondered how much the others had been told about her. Historically, a shifter was only as safe as their secret. Catalina hated walking into situations where other people had more intel about her than she did about them.

Just a reminder, Mitch Grayson is Luke's uncle—he isn't as gifted, but he's still a force to be reckoned with.

Israel's warning floated through her mind, and Cooper's lack of response let her know the message had been sent directly to her. *Interesting.* Grayson wouldn't be a problem if she paid attention. Having grown up with an empath who was a magical put her way ahead in the game she suspected would be played at dinner.

Second piece of unsolicited advice—don't wear panties. They weren't kidding about it being a line you don't want to cross.

Ewww. Just ewww. The last thing she wanted to think about was her brother giving her panty advice. Geez, Louise, how embarrassing. As Israel's quiet laughter faded to the back of her mind, Cat realized she'd zoned out long enough for the Lamonts to leave the two of them alone.

"Chatting with your brother, Princess?" She must have looked surprised because he had the audacity to roll his eyes. "Darlin', the crackle of electricity is unmistakable. The issue is, I wasn't included, so I would like to be briefed now."

Taking a deep breath, Cat gave herself a moment to consider his position and ignore his sudden slip into Southern slang. When he went good ol' boy on her, she needed to tread carefully.

Honestly, she understood his frustration and doubted Israel had deliberately excluded him. Heck, one of them had to keep up the conversation with the Lamonts. She told Cooper everything Israel said, including the warning about panties at dinner, and watched as his brows furrowed.

"I was going to make a rude comment about his warning being inappropriate until I realized I probably would have done the same for Lakyn under similar circumstances." She tilted her head, wondering what he meant by the circumstances, but his only response was a grin. "Zach said they left something in the closet for you to wear tonight. I'm going to check and make sure it will work, then make a call while you take a quick shower."

Catalina frowned. She wasn't thrilled he and Zach were deciding what she should wear to dinner. Sighing to herself, Cat let it go. As a member of a large family, she'd learned to choose her battles.

An hour later, Catalina walked down the sweeping staircase beside Cooper, wondering what the hell she'd gotten herself into. The voices coming from the dining room were boisterous, and she felt herself relax when laughter seemed to be on the menu. As they passed the front door, a stunning brunette stepped into the massive foyer. The man following her had to be close to six and a half feet tall, not counting the felt cowboy hat settled on his head.

"Sweetheart, I have no idea how you manage to out-pace me in those damned heels, but I surely do enjoy the view." The man extended his hand to Cooper, introducing himself as Trace Bartell, his wife smiled warmly, then turned to Catalina.

"It's great to meet you. I'm Tori Bartell. I've heard a lot about your jewelry designs and can hardly wait until some of the pieces make their way to the ShadowDance Club." The men were already chatting about security in the surrounding area, making Cat wonder if she should go back upstairs to get her laptop.

"Tori, let the pretty lady enjoy her dinner before you start shopping. I promise we'll give you a few minutes to chat before we head over the club."

"How far is the club?" Catalina wasn't sure she had enough energy for a club night. A bit of fun during dinner was one thing—a full-blown scene lasting until the wee hours of the morning was another.

"It's just next door, Ms. Adler. Tori and I don't get to play as often as we'd like, so we're looking forward to this evening. I want you to know my ranch hands and I will be on the lookout for strangers." His enormous hand wrapped around her elbow, stopping her before they stepped into the dining room. "I know your safety, and that of those like you depends on secrecy. You can trust us, Catalina, I want you to know your secrets are safe here. I have instructed the men who work for me they are to refrain from shoot-ing any wolf until further notice. They believe you are studying them and would be upset if one was harmed." Tori leaned forward and grinned.

"My husband and Master is brilliant. He didn't lie, and it will help keep you safe. I'm always impressed with the ways he manages to keep his integrity and have a gloriously perfect ass." Tori threw her head back and laughed at her own joke, although it was entirely possible some of her amusement was in response to the stunned look on Catalina's face. Trace closed his eyes, his chin dropping to his chest as he shook his head.

"I swear, I can't take her anywhere anymore. Hell, maybe that's the problem—she doesn't get away the from ranch often enough. If this keeps up, I'm going to have to send her to one of those fancy finishing schools to get my shy, prim, and proper subbie back."

Catalina giggled. It was painfully obvious this was familiar banter for the couple, and she admired their easy rapport.

Walking into the dining room, Catalina grinned at the man leaning against the fireplace mantle and the stunning woman at his side. Moving swiftly to the couple, the beauty known to the world as Ilaina, pulled her into a warm embrace.

"Catalina, it's wonderful to see you. Noah and I were thrilled to hear you'd be in the area for a while." Cat had worked with Noah Drummond and knew he'd retired from operative work a couple of years earlier. When she turned to the man who always reminded her of a California surfer, she extended her hand, but he shook his head, laughing as he pulled her into a bone-crushing hug.

"I don't think so, sweetness. Damn, it's good to see you. I heard about your kidnapping after the fact." Stepping back until she was arms-length, Noah's knowing gaze moved over her, and Cat grinned as his thoughts filtered through her mind. *She looks healthy enough, all things considered. Still going to get her to pose for me. Maybe Cooper can help me convince her.*

"It's good to see you, too. Ilaina, you are a vision as always. Noah, you've been after me to pose for you for longer than I can remember. I believe we might be able to negotiate something. I want to talk to you about shooting the advertising promos for my new line of erotic jewelry." His broad smile was all the answer she needed.

"Do you have models in mind, or are you open to suggestions?" His eyes not only flickered briefly in his wife's direction but was moving around the room. "Real women. Real submissives, along with their Doms, would be perfect. Let me pull my ideas into something resembling a presentation, then we'll talk. Stop by the studio when you get a chance. Alex and Zach can tell you how to access the tunnel. It's close by and ends inside the secured perimeter of the warehouse."

"The studio is amazing, Catalina. You'll be impressed with what Noah's done with the place." Ilaina's voice was filled with pride, making Cat grin.

She could remember when the world-famous model did everything humanly possible to avoid Noah. Strong, warm arms encircled her, the scent of her mate making her entire body respond. Heat moved through her veins as her pussy flooded with cream.

"Mitch Grayson is watching you, Princess. I don't know what you're thinking, but the corners of his mouth are tilting up, so I'm assuming you're focused on how anxious you are for me to fuck you into a coma." Without being told who she was looking for, Catalina's eyes zeroed in on the man in question. She was grateful for Cooper's distraction, but she was ready to meet this challenge head-on, and it looked like she wasn't going to have to wait long.

"It's nice to finally meet you, Ms. Adler. I've heard a lot about you from my nephew, Luke."

"I saw you at Crystal's christening, but you left before we were introduced." Cat hadn't found out until later who he was, but she'd remembered how intently he'd watched her.

"I remember. You are right, I was watching you, but more importantly, I was listening to you. It seems you were longing to run through the desert mountains surrounding Luke and Brooklyn's home." Mitch was right, she had been thinking about how fun it would be to feel the cool mountain air moving through her thick fur. "Your secrets are safe with me. I have no desire to hurt you or your family. I suspect your brother cautioned you about me, but you can let those warnings fall on deaf ears." Catalina felt herself relax as he turned, motioning the woman who'd been standing with him to join them. "Baby, I'd like to introduce you to our honored guests, Catalina Adler and Cooper Hicks." The vivacious redhead extended her hand before Mitch could finish.

"It's great to finally meet you. I'm Rissa. I have a small salon inside the club. I hope you'll stop in. We'll have tea, you can show me pictures of your niece and nephews." The two of them fell into an easy conversation about the growing Adler family. Another man, this one, as tall as Trace Bartell, with the most electric blue eyes Catalina had ever seen, stepped up to Rissa and pressed his lips to hers.

"Come on, Love, it's time for dinner." Quick introductions as they walked to the table revealed he was the second of Rissa's two husbands, Bryant Davis.

Oh, snap. I hope he and Mitch will consider joining their wife for Noah's photoshoot. The contrast of blue and chocolate-brown eyes with Rissa's red hair and pearlescent skin will light up in photos.

Mitch laughed out loud as he slapped Cooper on the back. "She is everything you described and more, man. Her mind spins a thousand miles a minute—there's no doubt she and Brooklyn are sisters." The two men laughed as Rissa giggled at what must have been a shocked expression spreading over Cat's face.

"Don't try to figure it out… you'll just make yourself crazy. Doms complain about submissives sticking together like glue, but they are just as bad or worse. I swear their penchant for sharing information would put Google to shame."

Cat hadn't spent a lot of time at Prairie Winds—there'd actually been several times when she wondered how she could continue justifying the steep membership fee—but she had attended often enough to have heard Rissa's comment echoed among the submissives. She found it interesting the observation was the same whether the submissive was talking about Doms or Dommes.

"Wow, is that the dress Zach left for you? Holy crap on a cactus, it covers your pink bits. You probably wouldn't want to drop anything or reach for something on the top shelf, but still…" Katarina tapped a French-tipped nail against her lower lip, studying what Catalina was convinced was a shirt, masquerading as a dress. The petite blonde looked better than she had an hour ago, with more color in her cheeks, and her blue eyes were sparkling. Whatever *set her world back to rights*, as Mama Adler used to say, seemed to have been effective.

"I'll explain it to you later, Princess." Cooper leaned over her shoulder, his whispered words wafting over the shell of her ear, sending a shiver of desire skittering up her spine. He pulled her back against his chest, and she felt what she was certain was a growl deep in his chest. She wondered if their mating would eventually alter his DNA enough to allow him to shift. Knowing it didn't always happen, wishing for it seemed like too much to ask, so she'd tried to put it out of her mind, but now it was all she could think about.

Once everyone was seated, the first thing Cat noticed was the way all the submissives were sitting with their knees spread wide, their bare feet hooked around the outside of their chair's front legs. *Where the heck are their shoes?* Looking around the table, she noted the raised brows of a couple of the Doms and an indulgent smile on Noah's face.

"When in Rome, Catalina," was all Noah said, but it was enough. Cooper had been busy chatting with Alex and hadn't noticed the sudden tension until he heard Noah's warning. With Cooper's attention turned to her, Catalina sighed before adopting a similar position. Cool air drifted over her heated sex, and she smiled to herself when the incantation she mentally recited began adding length to her skirt in small measures.

Cooper nodded his approval before returning to his conversation with Alex. Looking around the table, Mitch

Grayson's eyes twinkled in amusement. He gave her a quick nod of what looked like amusement.

"Please tell me you brought sketches of your new line." Katarina's words brought her mind back to business.

"I brought my laptop. I'm looking forward to showing you what I've designed."

"Ian tells me the two of you are working together. Do you have any of the security pieces ready to go?" Zach's question was followed by silence. Everyone at the table stopped talking—hell, they were barely breathing—and Cat wanted to shake her head. Why did the mention of Ian McGregor's name always have this effect on people?

"There are a couple of pieces ready. The microchips are powerful domestically, but we don't have enough coverage for them to be reliable out of the country. Ian is reluctant to sell them until the networking issue is resolved, and I agree with him." Listening to Zach's thoughts was easy. It was a relief to know his interest was genuine. Running her fingers through her hair, Catalina was hit with a strange wave of sadness at the realization she'd become so cynical.

"Yes. Oh, God, yes." Katarina's words had Cat turning to find out what she'd missed during her short mental road trip.

"Kitten, you're soaked Damn, that's hot."

Looking down through the glass table, it was easy to see Zach's fingers sliding between the swollen petals of his wife's pussy. When they disappeared, Katarina's head fell back, her breathing so shallow, Cat wondered how long the other woman would be able to stay in her seat. Studying Katrina's expression as she transitioned through multiple levels of pure sensuality made Cat wonder how the changes would look on film.

If Noah can capture those expressions for our advertising blitz, we'll make a fucking fortune.

Mitch Grayson's bark of laughter startled Catalina but didn't appear to have any effect on Katarina. Zach leaned over his wife, sealing his lips over hers, capturing what Catalina suspected would have been a scream. Within seconds, Katarina's entire body became so lax it looked like she might indeed slide right out of her chair. Looking around, Cat found it intriguing how the others were still chatting amiably, seemingly oblivious to the porno skit playing out a few feet away. Alex Lamont smiled indulgently at his wife, gave his brother a stiff nod, then resumed his conversation with Cooper.

"I don't think you will have any trouble explaining your advertising strategy to Noah. He seemed as captivated with Katarina's facial expressions as you were."

Turning to Mitch, Cat couldn't help but smile. "You've surprised me. Luke is much more clandestine with his ability to eavesdrop."

"My nephew may be more gifted, but I'm wiser." His half-grin and easy-going manner put her at ease. "I learned a long time ago to be upfront with my observations. If that's impossible for some reason, I close down the channel of communication. I try to surround myself with individuals who are aware of my special ability. For the most part, they are comfortable with me because they know I'm not going to… what is the expression Betsy uses?"

"Throw them under the bus?" Rissa shrugged before adding, "Your lovely daughter has too many expressions for me to be certain, but I'm guessing that's the one you're talking about."

"Uh oh, if she's being referred to as your lovely daughter, I'm betting Sweet E is in trouble with her mama." Bryant Davis's laughter made his blue eyes look like they'd been lit from the inside by some unseen spark turned deep-sea inferno.

"She's a hot mess, and the two of you indulge her every whim. I swear she is going to grow up thinking every man she meets is going to fall at her feet in adoration." Turning to Catalina, she shrugged. "I love her to death, but I swear she makes me insane. Do all daughters turn their mothers into shrews? I feel like I'm biting at her heels all the time."

"My mother had ten kids, but I don't ever remember her being a shrew. I doubt yours will remember you that way either." Leaning back in her chair, Cat realized an eerie silence had fallen around her. As odd as it seemed to her, people often seemed interested in how a family with ten children managed—how the simple day-to-day operation of the household remained functional. "My mom made it seem easy, even though I know it wasn't. We were a wild group, and I suspect she used magic more often than any of us knew."

"My parents knew yours. They were all friends when the oil boom was in its infancy. She told me how remarkable they were." Alex's strong voice sounded from her other side, making Catalina return her attention to him.

"I met your parents at a party at Ian and Callie's. I don't remember the occasion, but despite how brief our encounter was, I've never forgotten the sense of peace and confidence that seemed to surround your mom, and your dad seemed like a gentleman from another era. I remember thinking how he reminded me of my own dad." There was an awkward silence Catalina hated. It didn't happen as often now as it had when her parents had first died, but it still felt like she was being suffocated as the air around them thickened with unease. She'd learned quickly, most people were damned uncomfortable talking with victims' families.

"Earlier, Mitch said something about us being on the same page with advertising shots. Were you watching the expressions on Katarina's face?" Cat was grateful for Noah's change of subject and sensed the others at the table felt the same way. Glancing at the other woman, Cat couldn't hold back her grin at Katarina's blush.

"A single shot of a real woman lost in her lover's touch will sell more kink jewelry than a thousand celebrities holding one of the pieces as they read from a damned teleprompter. And no offense, Ilaina, but some of your peers would be lucky to read anything above a dull third-grade level."

"You're preaching to the choir, sister. It drove me insane to work with people who didn't like to read books because they were tired of looking up what the words meant. Several of them were being tutored through high school on location. I have no idea how they'd even managed to get *into* high school, but I suspect the late-night visits by sponsors were a large part of their academic success."

"So beautiful, yet so cynical." Noah's taunting drew glares from the submissives around the table and chuckles from the Doms. "Before I start a riot, perhaps we should move this party to the club."

Looking down at her plate, Cat was shocked to find it empty. Holy hat-racks, when had she eaten?

"Catalina and I are going to skip the club tonight." Cooper grasped Cat's hand, the familiar sizzle of electricity between them moved through her slower than usual. "We've had a long day of travel, and both need to rest."

If you're lucky, we might make it all the way into our suite before I shove my cock so deep in your heat, it will be impossible to tell where you end and I begin.

Promises, promises, mate.

She felt the air around them shift and knew her challenge wasn't going to be ignored. When Cooper bent at the waist, pushing his shoulder into her torso, Catalina gasped when he lifted her effortlessly into the air. Walking swiftly from the room, he flipped the remaining hem still hovering over the top of the ass and slapped his hand down on her bare skin before she had a chance to protest.

His growled command to stay still made her want to comment on his Neanderthal performance but connecting to his thoughts stilled her tongue. His performance had essentially cut off any protests from the others about their decision to skip the club. She was grateful for their quick exit, but the shouts of encouragement from the other Doms as Cooper climbed the stairs was damned embarrassing all the same.

Chapter Fourteen

Two days later

D ARK, MISTY SHADOWS slithered between the trees, the
air heavy with ill-will. The stories Catalina had heard
since arriving on ShadowDance Mountain spoke of joyous
celebrations honoring the majestic beauty of the surrounding, marking the changing seasons, and honoring various
phases of the moon. Nothing in those old tales mentioned
malevolence, and Cat knew the darkness was waiting for
her.

Alex and Zach Lamont had shared stories about the
Native American folklore attributed to the mountain's
interesting name. They'd regaled her with colorful tales
about spirits dancing in celebration of the full moon, the
end of winter, and bountiful harvest. Tonight, those
thankful dancers remained hidden, even when they had to
know the only way to banish darkness was with light.
Evidently. even the longest passed spirit knew survival
trumped a missed opportunity to dance in the silvery
moonlight.

Catalina stood in the center of the small meadow, letting the moon's luminescent light sparkle as it seemed to

dance along the tips of her fur. She wasn't certain how she knew, but she was secure in the knowledge nothing could touch her in this spot. A familiar sense of protection always wrapped itself around her anytime she stood in the moonlight—the feeling was one of her first childhood memories. Years later, her mother explained the moon's magic was as powerful as the earth's, and being chosen by either was an honor for any magical.

Brighten Adler had cautioned Catalina to remain grateful for the gifts she received, no matter how challenging they might become. As a young girl, she hadn't understood how magical gifts could be considered anything other than a blessing, but as she'd grown older, it became clear. Sometimes the price you paid for those special skills was damned high.

When she'd first arrived, she remained hidden in the underbrush. Crouching in the thick pine scrub, watching and waiting felt dangerous, so she'd moved out into the open. The temperature dropped so suddenly, Cat's wolf felt the shift, the sudden chill in the air making her hackles stand up. Danger lurked all around her, but she sensed the threat was being held back by a force beyond her senses.

Trust your instincts, my darling daughter. Stay in the moonlight and return to the Lamonts home. Help awaits.

Catalina knew her heart skipped several beats when her father's voice moved through her mind. She couldn't begin to count the number of times she'd prayed the Universe would let her hear the deep timbre of his voice one more time. Frozen in the moment, Catalina knew she should be moving but didn't want to break the spell. Something deep inside her wanted to believe he'd speak again if she remained perfectly still.

Catalina, get your ass in gear! I don't know what's going on up there, but your parents are yelling at me, your damned brother is pitching a fit, and my uncle is threatening to send out a fucking search party. What the fuck. Get moving.

If Cat hadn't been in her wolf, she'd have laughed out loud. Luke and Brooklyn lived in New Mexico. Cat bet her brother-in-law was sitting in what her sister affectionately referred to as the bat cave, inundated by telepathic communication. The man was off-the-chart gifted and dealt with a tsunami of information that would drive most people to drink themselves into a stupor.

Catalina had seen her brother, Israel, swear he was going to lose his mind in crowded rooms when they were kids. He'd eventually learned to shut down the noise in his head, but none of the empaths she knew would shut down any line of communication when someone they cared about was in trouble.

Running the barely discernable small animal paths she'd found in the forest, Catalina was able to avoid the predators the Lamonts had warned her about but staying hidden from magical threats was much more difficult. Twice she felt the icy chill of a nearby spirit, but she hadn't gotten the impression they meant her harm. The closer she got to the Lamonts' house, the safer she felt. Unfortunately, Cat knew it was going to be important to explore beyond the point where she'd been tonight. Whatever had been out there wasn't going to go away until it was dealt with—and she was tired of running.

KATARINA STOOD IN the shadows holding Catalina's clothes. She'd followed their guest outside but had been too far behind and missed the woman shifting into a wolf. Determined to see for herself how the process worked, Kat stayed so still, she was barely breathing. It wasn't her new friend who was her main concern—it was Alex and Zach. God only knew how they'd react if they found out she was waiting to spy on a guest. As if she'd jinxed herself by thinking about them, a thick arm wrapped around her torso and pulled her back against a well-muscled chest.

"What are you doing, Kitten?" She wasn't fooled by Zach's whiskey smooth voice—he wasn't pleased.

"Holy fat fairies, you scared me." She felt his chest shake and knew he was laughing at her. "I don't know why you ask me questions you already know the answer to, but I'm staying right here until I get to see how this whole shifting thing works. Cooper said there are other magicals in this area, but he wasn't aware of any other shifters." Looking over her shoulder, she wasn't surprised to see Zach's expression change from frustration to thoughtful interest.

"I know the Stone sisters are considered white witches. They've both told me their magic is based on the natural laws of the Universe. Their store is an interesting place to visit. They are both characters—intelligent, ornery as sin, and funny."

"Have you ever seen them perform magic?" Without waiting for him to answer, she plunged full speed ahead,

"Dang, I'll bet you have. Why didn't I know about them? Swear to all things holy, I live under a rock."

"Sweetness, you have four wild as the wind kids, two husbands, in-laws who adore you but regularly request your help for their favorite charitable causes, and a business that has grown by leaps and bounds—I'm not sure when you'd be able to fit in traipsing around the mountains, checking out magical shops."

When he put it that way, Kat didn't feel so much like a slacker. Neither of her husbands had ever been anything but supportive of all her activities... unless they thought she was pushing herself too hard, then all bets were off.

Before she could respond, the largest wolf Katarina had ever seen ran across the courtyard. The magnificent beast slowed suddenly, sensing it wasn't alone. Kat couldn't hold back her squeal of delight.

"Damn, damn, and double-damn. You are gorgeous. I'm sorry if I scared you. It's Zach's fault. He's all big and grinchy looking, but he's just snooping on my... um, well, I guess he was checking on my attempt to spy on you. I picked up your clothes so they wouldn't get dew on them. Can I watch you shift? We can make Zach look the other way, but to be honest, he's seen about a gazillion naked women, so you probably shouldn't worry about that part. Cooper told me you can shift in clothes, but it shreds them, so I sort of pieced together you'd be naked. He didn't mean to throw your bare self under the bus or anything." Pausing to take a breath, Kat shook her head.

"Frack, I'm babbling. I know it isn't nice to spy, but I couldn't help myself. Zach should probably get points for his claim that he was checking on me, even though that's pretty darned lame if you ask me. Oh... wait. I know, I'll give you a huge discount on the web-designs if you let me watch." Katarina had never been this close to a wolf before, so she didn't have anything to compare it to, but damned if it didn't look like the animal was smiling.

Bones started shortening, the thick fur appeared to be disappearing back into her skin, and the wolf's long snout was retreating. Within a few seconds, Catalina Adler stood before them, naked as the day she was born. Grinning at the two of them, she held out her hand for the clothing Katarina clutched to her chest.

"Can I have my clothes? Shifters are by nature comfortable being naked, but it's damned cold now that I'm a human again. I might have lived in New York for several years, but I didn't walk around outside in what Ms. Brighten Adler called my *altogether*." Pulling on the clothes Katarina handed her, Cat smiled at the woman's wide eyes.

"Holy shit... tzu." Katarina's attempted save seemed to amuse Zach.

"Kitten, ordinarily I'd swat your ass for that slip, but I was thinking the same thing, so it would be hypocritical for me to call you out."

Catalina was pleased to see Zach's eyes never left her face. She'd meant what she said about being comfortable in her own skin, but she appreciated his respect.

"Let's go inside. I don't know about you ladies, but I could use a stiff drink."

Cooper met them at the back door, his expression seeming to shift subtly from concern to amusement as he listened to Katarina's string of questions.

"How old were you when you first discovered you

could change into a wolf? Did your friends at school know? Can all your sisters and brothers change? Do they change into wolves or something else? Do some people change into other animals? Can anyone change into more than one animal? Have you ever been shot at?"

"*Katarina*. Take a breath, love." Alex Lamont's sharp command brought them all up short. Cooper pulled her against his side, his scent soothing her in a way nothing else could. Lying side by side in bed late last night, he'd asked if mating had changed her. Her answer seemed to surprise him.

"Your scent affects me in ways I didn't expect. It can launch me into the deep end of arousal so quickly, my head spins, but it also calms me when I'm struggling with all the changes in my life. The small shifts in your body chemistry from the DNA enhancements taking place are noticeable to me, and I suspect your sense of smell is becoming stronger. I know your eyesight has improved because you have seen things in this dark room you wouldn't have noticed before."

His arm tightened around her, bringing her back to the moment as he spoke against her ear, "I swear your mind works at the speed of light, Princess. For the record, you're right. I notice significant improvements to my senses every day. The changes have been remarkable." He'd spoken so quietly, the words would have been impossible for the Lamonts to hear—even if they hadn't been talking a mile a minute among themselves.

"Sorry if I overwhelmed you with questions, but seeing you shift was the most amazing thing I've ever seen. It was equal parts awesome and terrifying. Well, it was the snapping and crackling of bones shifting that was terrifying, but you get the idea." Katarina's eyes sparkled with intelligence, and Cat grinned at the other woman before accepting the drink Zach handed her. Settling on the sofa in front of the fire, she snickered at Katarina's hopeful expression.

"I'll answer your questions under two conditions. First, everything we discuss stays in this room, or at least you refrain from discussing it with anyone other than your husbands. Second, your offer for a bargain on my website design is still on the table."

Alex and Zach both leaned their heads back and laughed.

"She'd probably do it for free to get answers, Catalina." Zach grinned from his seat on the other side of the heavy wood table at the center of the seating area facing the largest fireplace Catalina had ever seen in a private home. "I had the feeling you returned to the house in a hurry, and I'd be interested to know why."

Zach's astute observation surprised her. She knew he'd been in the Special Forces and expected him to be perceptive, but this was more than a simple observation. Explaining what she'd felt, then heard, Cat wondered if the trio would think she'd lost her mind.

Remember, they deal with Mitch Grayson, so they understand and respect empathic gifts.

Thanks for the reminder. I'm still reeling a bit from having them waiting for me when I returned.

Shifting in front of Katarina and Zach Lamont had been a huge leap of faith, one she wouldn't have ordinarily considered. For the next hour, Catalina answered every question the three of them posed. When the answers weren't easy to put into words, she was impressed with their ability to grasp the complex nuances of magic.

"Do you think there are other shifters in this area? We've met several of your siblings over the years and know they are considered shifters, but I have to tell ya', *knowing* and *seeing* are two entirely different things."

"Who was in the control room when Catalina returned?" Cooper's question felt like someone suddenly dropped a truckload of bricks on her chest. Holy fucking hell, how had she managed to get her head so far up her ass, she'd failed to consider all the security monitoring equipment she knew was in place? The Lamont's property was a virtual fortress—one of the reasons she'd been sent here. Slip-ups like her lapse in thinking got operatives killed. It wasn't like she was a damned beginner—fucking hell, she knew better.

"Mitch and I were the only ones up there when you left and returned, Catalina. We'll make certain we warn you when other members of our security team are on shift. Your safety is our number one concern, so there will certainly be times you won't have any expectation of privacy outside your own suite. There are few blind spots." Alex looked at Katarina and raised a brow, challenging her to argue. "I'm sure our lovely wife will be happy to show you the ones she's discovered. Keep your phone on you. We'll text if she takes you to one of the coveted private spots we've recently covered."

"Wait. What? Are you fixing them? As in wiring every inch of this place for sight and sound? How's a girl supposed to pop a squat in the woods? Well, if that doesn't beat all. I tell you, the world is going to hell in a handbasket."

Catalina didn't know Katarina Lamont well enough to decide if the pretty blonde was kidding, serious, or if her mini-rant was something in-between.

"Love, I'd better not *hear or see* anything remotely related to you *popping a squat* outside. If your bare ass is going to be recorded for posterity, my brother or I better be present, or those high-definition videos will be the least of your worries." Alex's warning was spoken so sincerely, Cat started to wonder if the whole group was serious.

How can they be so security conscious and not know their wife if peeing with the bears in the woods?

Cooper's bark of laughter brought her back to the moment, and she turned to look at the man who was now her mate. "Princess, Katarina was trying to break the tension, and Alex is playing along."

"Playing along? But he seems so much like Kyle West, how can he be playing along?"

"She's got you there, Alex." Katarina burst into a fit of giggles despite her husbands' glares. Waving Alex off when he started to speak, Kat continued, "Yeah, yeah, I know. Swats. I'm going to pay… won't be able to sit comfortably for days. But you know what? Watching the largest wolf I've ever seen change into our houseguest was worth every stinging blow."

The room fell silent for several seconds while Katarina's Doms' mouths fell open. Cat could feel Cooper shaking with the laughter trying desperately to hold back. Catalina might have been able to keep a straight face if the other woman hadn't given her a saucy wink. The simple gesture tipped the scales, sending Cat into a fit of giggles. Laughter erupted around the room, providing much-needed relief from the pressure of the past few days.

It took several minutes for everyone to settle back into the conversation. Cat was relieved to feel a new sense of calm settle over them as conversations took several turns around children, growing tensions as political changes were implemented around the world, and the safety concerns Catalina faced. When their chat turned back to Cat, Alex and Zach both leaned forward, elbows resting on their knees, and fingers steepled loosely together.

Remarkable. Even their gestures are mirror images.

Catalina answered the Lamonts' questions about her captivity. They'd apologized for the intrusive nature of the conversation, explaining they hoped the *new eyes theory* would come into play. She'd worked independently so much of her career, it was a concept she understood but rarely had the opportunity to employ. Bringing in someone new to take a fresh look and hopefully ask enough thought-provoking questions to spark an answer was an interesting blend of their military and business backgrounds.

Through it all, Katarina sat back, listening, and watching the interplay between her husbands and guests. She rarely contributed to the conversation, but Catalina could practically hear the other woman's mind spinning. A sudden shift in the energy of the room made the hair on Catalina's arms stand on end. Returning her focus to Katarina, Cat watched as the air around her crackled with brightly colored sparks. Katarina's aura—something Cat didn't ordinarily see—changed colors quickly. Two things struck Catalina at once—first, it was obvious her own magical abilities were growing exponentially, and second, her new friend had just had an epiphany.

"Have you considered that Catalina isn't the only target? Who will run to her aid if they come for her again?" Without missing a beat, she answered her own question. "It's not a secret how Cooper feels about her—after all, they're mated, right? Anyway, anyone wanting to use Catalina's magical skill for nefarious purposes would have to go through Cooper. Once you eliminated him, you'd face Cameron Barnes. Now, I don't know Mr. Barnes, but his reputation precedes him. Apparently, he's a bit of a hardass as a Dom and something of a legend as an intelligence officer."

Her husbands stared at her in disbelief, but the woman waved them off. "Don't worry, I didn't pick the pathetic lock on your desk and rummage through your files. There is more than enough information available on the... well, the internet. You can find all sorts of interesting things if you take the time to look."

"Love, if you've been looking around the dark web, you'll have bought more trouble than you bargained for."

"Kitten, we had a deal."

"I didn't renege on our deal. Katarina Lamont has not been on the dark web." Catalina wanted to laugh out loud at Kat's obvious devious game of semantics. There wasn't a chance in hell the men were going to fall for it, but it was amusing all the same. "I think Catalina's magic is the target, and the piss-widget who tried to set them up is a tool of the dark magicals. Setting Cooper and Barnes up was just a fast way to get them out of the way." Katarina's casual shrug belied the brilliant insight she'd brought to the discussion.

At first glance, Katarina Lamont looked like a woman from a 1960s sitcom—blonde, beautiful, and ditzy. Cat would bet it was a stereotype Katarina dealt with often. From what she'd observed, Katarina was smart as a whip, and Catalina looked forward to working with her.

Catalina, Cooper, and Cam had all considered the possibility there was a covert group within the American intelligence community targeting Cam and Cooper, but no one was sure why. Katarina's fresh eyes had done more than offer another perspective—the sudden clarity of the mystery surrounding the list made Cat's head spin.

"Your names were on the list. On the one hand, I knew it had to be true. It was the only thing that made sense. But..." Catalina rubbed her open palm over her forehead, the pulsing in her head as the memories flooded back in, making her head pound. "That's why I blocked out actually seeing them written on the list. I knew it wasn't true. It couldn't be true. But they thought I'd walk away from you if I believed you'd betrayed our country. Not only would you be locked up, but I'd cut all ties to you and be more vulnerable. They weren't angry I wasn't giving them all the names. Hell, they already had the list of real traitors. This was all about making certain I was isolated."

She hadn't been able to remember the interrogations she'd endured at the hands of her captors—nothing about that time existed aside from the pain. Catalina knew she'd fueled their anger but hadn't understood why... until now. The hair on her arms stood on end, and she automatically sat ramrod straight, poised for whatever was about to happen. Cooper reacted a split second later, but the reason for the energy making the entire room shimmer was already sitting in a nearby wingback chair.

"Brigitte, it's nice to see you. Interesting entrance." For some reason, Alex's calm response struck Catalina as funny. Laughing out loud it wasn't long before Kat joined her, the two of them cackling like loons. Through it all, the only thing Catalina heard was Gigi's steady voice.

"I'd be insulted if I wasn't so damned relieved to see her smile again. My niece has been riding my ass about being heavy-handed with her new in-laws—can you believe it?"

"Baffling." Sarcasm practically dripped from Zach Lamont's tone, but Gigi ignored him.

"I'm not surprised to learn you are a magical, but I'm pissed I didn't figure it out on my own. I'll bet your dark... umm, I mean, lower-level internet profile is virtually non-existent. Damn and double damn. How did I miss this? Why do I get the feeling I'm the only one who is surprised?" The petite blonde looked from Alex to Zach, then back to Alex. Katarina's eyes narrowed in a virtual dare as she waited for her men to deny they'd already suspected Gigi Stafford was a witch.

"I doubt they had conclusive proof, but it seems unlikely they hadn't been briefed. Their network is *extensive,* and in my experience, men are terrible gossips—far worse than women."

Cat wasn't sure it had been Brigitte's intention to break the tension with humor, but it had worked like a charm. One of the things she'd learned from her sister-in-law, Charlotte, was to expect the unexpected when it came to the Stafford family.

Chapter Fifteen

BRIGITTE STAFFORD HADN'T planned to reveal herself to the Lamonts but staying hidden in the shadows burned energy—a lot of energy—and the power would be better utilized in other ways. Invisibility was one of the magical skills she shared with her niece, Charlotte. It was easy for short periods of time, but the amount of concentration required was exhausting. Charlotte's ability to shimmer until she vanished would grow stronger as she aged. Gigi felt a pang of sympathy for Charlotte's son—the poor kid was never going to get away with anything.

"I want to hear about what happened in the clearing." The Magic Council was trying to determine who was responsible for the full-out effort to move Catalina's skill set to the other end of the spectrum. She was growing more powerful so quickly, even she hadn't fully registered all the changes. Shifting Catalina's loyalty to the dark side would tip the delicately balanced scale between magical good and evil. Listening to her detailed description of what she'd heard and felt, Brigitte was pleased to know Cat recognized the importance of the way her body reacted to the malicious energy.

"Keep in mind, these forces are trying to recruit you.

What happened after your kidnapping was the work of a few people who hadn't been vetted. You were never supposed to be mistreated, and if Cooper hadn't killed them, they'd have suffered a worse fate at the hands of the dark magicals wanting to bring her under their wing."

"Vetted? Seriously? They almost killed her." Brigitte could hear the utter disbelief and frustration in Cooper's voice. One of the facets of magic nonmagicals struggled with was the community's laissez-faire attitude when it came to interfering with fate's purpose. Gigi knew surviving the physical and emotional damage inflicted by Catalina's captors hadn't been easy. The young witch wasn't at the end of the dark tunnel yet, but she could finally see a flickering light like a promise-filled beacon at the other end. *In the end, we are all products of our experiences—both good and bad. People will never truly appreciate the light unless they've experienced darkness.*

"I understand your frustration, Cooper. Fate can be a real pain in the ass."

"Preach, sister." Katarina's whispered words made Gigi grin.

"I find it interesting two sets of twins, deeply immersed in the world of kink, all members of elite military forces, separated by several states—which eliminates environmental influences—yet the four of you have chosen women who are remarkably similar in looks and personality." Drumming her fingers on the wooden arm of the chair she'd chosen, Gigi tilted her head to the side, her gaze moving between Alex and Zach. "If I was interested in social psychology, I'd be studying the lot of you very closely." Shaking her head as to clear the lingering fog of being lost for a moment in curiosity, Brigitte smiled at Catalina.

"As I'm sure you have already noticed, your magical power is increasing at an accelerated rate. The good news is, you're going to find a lot of great applications for the skills. The bad news? There are other forces at work in the Universe that would enjoy harnessing your energy to further their own agenda."

"I KEEP TRYING to hear what you *aren't saying,* but it's just out of my reach. Help me out." Catalina was tired and wanted to cut to the chase. A couple of mind-melting orgasms and a few hours of sleep would do her a world of good, and those were being delayed by Brigitte dancing around whatever she'd come to say. *Damn, girl... get on with it. I know you didn't come here to chit-chat about social fucking psychology.*

"I don't know what you're thinking, but it seems there are empaths in your life who are damned amused. They've given me five minutes before you waltz out of here." Catalina would have been mortified if she hadn't had previous experience with Gigi's sense of humor. "Okay, here's what I want you to do. When you shift tomorrow to go exploring, run the perimeter. We're hoping you'll be able to tell us how they've gotten past the Lamonts' security and the extra layer the council has put in place."

Identical looks of frustration clouded Alex and Zach's faces, making Cat snicker. She'd bet they were not thrilled having the integrity of their security questioned. Having the council add their own safety measures without consulting them would have added insult to injury.

"Come on, Princess. I know you're beat. Let's let Alex and Zach chat with Brigitte while you and I head upstairs." Cooper had evidently gotten the same vibe, and she was more than happy to walk away from the discussion she knew was coming. As one of the older siblings in her family, Cat was rarely exempted from the difficult *chats*, so she was happy to step away from this one. It wasn't until they were outside Alex and Zach's office that Cat realized Katarina had followed them. Catalina must have looked surprised because the other woman shrugged.

"I didn't want to listen to my men whine about someone questioning their ability to protect you. Occasionally, I can manage to keep quiet, but my facial expressions always give me away." Her cheeks turned a sweet shade of pink at the admission, endearing her even more to Catalina. "I'm going to work on your website. Go on up and get some sleep. I don't usually have a lot of time when the kids aren't underfoot, and I hate to waste the chance to focus for more than three minutes." The petite blonde gave Cat a quick hug before turning in the direction of her office.

Katarina's office was a light-filled solarium originally belonging to her mother-in-law. The colorfully decorated space sat empty after the elder Lamonts moved to Denver. When Katarina returned to Colorado, Alex and Zach quickly updated the space into an office for her web-design business. Once their grandchildren arrived, Daniel and Catherine bought a house in the nearby town, so they'd be nearby and available to help without living too close for everyone's comfort. Catalina had commented how lucky her friend was to have such close family ties, then had been humbled when she realized how lucky she was as well. At that moment, Catalina decided to stop comparing her own blessings to those of her friends.

Blessings are one of those rare gifts that aren't diminished by sharing.

Cooper led her into their suite, and Cat blinked, surprised to find herself there. *Good grief, I can't believe I walked upstairs without being aware we were moving.*

"I'm torn between being thrilled you trust me enough to let me lead you around while you're completely lost in thought and terrified you allowed me to lead you without once considering where we were headed." Cooper's words might have stung if she hadn't understood exactly what he was saying—distraction was damned dangerous, and she knew better.

"Now that you've rejoined me... strip, Princess." Crossing his arms over his chest, feet shoulder-width apart, Cooper's stance made him look every bit the formidable Dom she knew him to be. Damn, why did he have to be so fucking hot? She'd always been attracted to him... even when she didn't want to be.

"If you are finished looking at me like I'm a damned snack..." He didn't need to finish. She knew all too well how adverse he was to being forced to repeat commands.

Without hesitating, Cat peeled off her clothes, tossing them onto a nearby chair. After traveling the world for years, she had a real issue with clothing being on the floor—too many creepy-crawlies on the floors of hotels for her comfort.

"You are awfully distracted. What do you think would

help you focus, Princess?"

There was no way she was answering what was so obviously a trick question. It might have been rhetorical, but the warning was clear, and she was damned well going to stay in the moment to avoid whatever solution his wickedly creative mind dreamed up. Standing perfectly still while he walked around her wasn't easy, but she recognized it as a test—one she didn't intend to fail. He was making certain she hadn't been injured during her rush to get back. His fingers trailed over the surface of her skin over her ribs, the slight touch waking up every nerve cell and sending a wave of goosebumps racing down her arm.

"You are beautiful. Your skin is flawless and so soft, I always feel like I'm caressing warm silk. I love the way the blush of arousal shifts from pale pink to the deep rose that matches the swollen petals of your labia when you're fully aroused."

His softly spoken words sent a rush of cream from her core as her heart rate kicked up. He'd once made her come using nothing but his voice. The man was lethal in so many ways. Leading her into the master bath, Cooper started the shower before stripping out of his own clothes.

"Come on. I want to play a game."

Oh, boy, her mate had spent too much time undercover in casinos and had learned too well how to ensure the *house* won.

When he switched the shower to the handheld, Cat felt her knees weaken. Pulses of water jetted from the device as his sinister smile made her nipples draw up into tight peaks. She watched as he adjusted the temperature and pressure, fiddling with the shower's complicated controls until he was satisfied.

"One foot on the bench, toes pointed to the wall." The position opened up her sex, leaving nothing to the imagination. When she complied, he slipped his fingers through her wet folds and smiled. "So slick... I love the way the earthy scent of your arousal fills the air, wrapping itself around me and making my cock stand at attention. Here are the rules, my lovely mate. You have twenty swats on the board. For every five seconds you hold back your orgasm, I'll deduct one." Propping his waterproof watch on a nearby ledge, she could see he'd already set it to countdown from one hundred. "Are you ready to play, Princess?"

Are you out of your ever-loving mind? I don't have a snowball's chance in hell of winning. Let's just cut straight to the wild, swinging from the chandelier sex. Cooper's smile told her he'd heard her silent response. She needed to remember how strong their telepathic communication was becoming. What would work for her if she found herself in danger could also work against her during a scene.

"Yes, Sir."

"I'm glad you chose to share the edited version of your response mate. It would have been a shame to add to your beginning total. Although I have to admit, I'm hoping you don't make it the entire one hundred seconds. I have been looking forward to paddling your lovely ass. Feeling your skin heat beneath my palm is hotter than hell."

Without warning, water pulsed directly to her clit, making Cat shriek in surprise. Her eyes moved to his watch, wondering how it was possible the numbers were counting down at a fucking snail's pace—the damned thing was in slow motion.

Catalina's body trembled so violently, her knees threatened to fold. If her legs gave out, she would drop to the tiled floor like a damned sack of sand. Her pulse pounded in her ears, and the thumping of their heartbeat sounded like the kettle drums of her high school orchestra. In an effort to distract herself, Cat thought back on how she'd loved the way the music swept her away. She hadn't been a member of the elite musical group, but she'd snuck into their rehearsal hall at every opportunity. Damn, those memories weren't enough to distract from the heat rolling through her veins like lava, scorching everything in its path. When Cooper was finally finished, he'd have reduced her to little more than a pile of ash.

Cooper moved the handheld shower closer. Two quick pulses of jetting water slammed into her aching clit before he pulled back for several beats. The lack of predictability ramped up her response to a level she hadn't been able to anticipate. Frantically trying to stem her body's rapid slide into arousal, Cat started reviewing the jeweled pieces she planned to request Noah to photograph first. When she'd talked to him earlier today, he assured her he'd cleared his schedule for two days next week. He planned to fly to Austin so they could decide which pieces to use in the final photoshoot.

"You're going to come for me, Princess. Your slick cream will wash over my fingers at the exact moment I dictate." He pressed a soft kiss of reassurance against her forehead, then grinned. "I'll take good care of you, mate. Are you ready to fly?" Cooper's chuckle broke her concentration, and when she moved her eyes to his watch, Cat groaned. How was it possible the damned thing still hadn't counted down to zero? Before she could pull in another breath, several things happened at once. Cooper stepped to her side, essentially caging her between his muscular chest and the warm tiled wall, and the water jet moved back to her clit as he grasped the globe of her ass and squeezed. "Your throaty scream of release is hotter than hell... damn, I love hearing you shout my name as passion blanks your mind. Come for me, Princess. Come now!"

Nothing could have held back the earth-shattering orgasm she knew was about to burst free. Heat erupted in her core in an explosion of mind-melting desire, unlike anything she'd ever experienced. Screaming his name as her knees gave way, Cat heard the clatter of the handheld device dropping to the floor, but it seemed a thousand miles away. Wave after wave of heat rolled over her, the pressure in her core making it difficult for her to refrain from shifting. She recognized the deep-seated feeling and knew Cooper had probably already noted the change in her scent. She had to have the worst timing in the history of shifters.

"Twenty seconds. That's four swats... perfect. Two on each cheek. Your ass is fucking spectacular, Catalina. The only thing I like more than looking at the perfectly rounded globes of your ass is seeing it glowing crimson as I shove my cock balls deep in your sweet pussy."

She sagged against him, wondering how long he would make her wait before... She heard the sharp slap of skin against skin a fraction of a second before she gasped. Pain danced over the surface of her skin, leaving a lingering sense of anticipation. The second swat lifted her up on her toes, the heat sinking in deep enough to set off another orgasm so strong, she barely felt the last two swats.

The feeling of being lifted was disorienting, but as soon as she felt her back pressing against the steam-warmed tile, Catalina instinctively wrapped her legs around his waist. His cock had no trouble finding its target, and the erotic burn of stretching tissues sent her tumbling over again. Cooper's groan was music to her ears.

"Your pussy is squeezing me so tight, I'm not going to last, Princess. Fuck me, the rippling of your vaginal walls is the sweetest torture in the world. You're pulling me deeper, your body telling me it never wants to let me go. Damn, Catalina, I'm going to spend the rest of my life ensuring you never regret belonging to me."

Catalina wanted to respond, wanted to reassure Cooper she planned to hold him to his word, but her brain was fried past the point of forming a coherent sentence. His thrusts were powerful, pushing his tip against her cervix time and again until Cat's mind blanked out completely. White lights exploded behind her eyelids, and her scream bounced off the walls of the shower before she felt herself sliding down into a silent, inky abyss.

KATARINA LOOKED UP in confusion when she heard someone enter her office. Ordinarily, the place held something close to sacred status when her family knew she was working. At her request, they'd installed a door with a clear glass window so everyone could see she was deep in her thoughts before they disturbed her. With two husbands and three children, uninterrupted time was a precious commodity. Demanding respect for her privacy was the only way she'd been able to build her business into the success it had become.

"Kitten?" Zach's question brought her back to the moment. Rubbing her tired eyes, Kat looked from him to the clock on the wall, blinking to bring the distant numbers into focus. Damn, had she really been working four hours without a break? The sun would be coming up in a couple of hours and she knew better than to skip sleep altogether. What had only been a minor inconvenience in her twenties was now damn near impossible to pull off. Not that she was complaining—her life was full to the brim, and she loved it, but pulling all-nighters was beyond her capabilities.

"I don't know. She didn't hear me walk in and has been staring at the clock for the past several seconds without responding. Hell, I caught myself watching the damned thing, wondering if it was going to start playing music and dance along the shelf."

She recognized the irritation in Zach's voice, but it took her several long seconds to notice Alex standing by his side. Returning her attention to the bank of computer screens lining her desk, Kat typed in a series of commands, saving her work and sending the system into sleep mode.

"Come." Taking Alex's outstretched hand, Kat started to stand only to realize how stiff her legs were after sitting in one position for so long. Teetering precariously, she tried to take a step, but the sudden tingling in her legs made the movement impossible.

"It's been a long time since we had to paddle your

sweet ass for not taking care of yourself, Kitten. What were you thinking working so late?"

"Everything was coming together, and I didn't want to jinx myself by not following through. I always think I'll remember what I was going to do, then the ideas evaporate before I can get back here and put it on paper." She was probably one of the few in her field who still used real paper in her office.

"I'm sending a delayed text to our parents, asking them to keep our hellions for a few more days. I know our four children are a handful."

"And when you add Jenna's..." Zach's chuckle held more truth than genuine amusement.

"If there are dark forces of magic lurking nearby, the last thing we need is their curious minds working overtime." Kat barely registered Alex's words, but thinking about the myriad of ways their children could cause trouble with magical forces was too terrifying to consider.

Their young science nerds, Danny and Christopher, would want to study the metaphysics of magic. Alexa, the youngest, would try to capture the scene on paper, sketching furiously to ensure she captured enough details to paint later. The real problem would be a Mary Catherine. Their oldest daughter was the heir apparent to Aunt Jenna's Warrior Fairy legacy. She was skilled in several types of martial arts but failed miserably when it came to recognizing her limits. Unfortunately, Mary Catherine also inherited her mother's unique ability to find trouble.

"Ordinarily, I'd feel like she was deliberately ignoring us, but this time I honestly think she is so tired, the lights are on, but no one is home." Zach kissed her forehead, holding her up while Alex undressed her. "I often wonder how Dad managed." Kat looked around, shocked to find herself standing in their bedroom.

"I have no idea. Marrying a brilliant woman presents an entire set of unique challenges. To be honest, I think our lovely wife is carrying the lion's share of the load around here. She manages the house, helps with staff, has built an extraordinarily successful business, and still manages to bring everything we could have ever dreamed of into our lives... and I'm not just referring to sex."

"Fuck. Now I feel like a damned slacker." Zach's comment made her smile. If there was one thing Alex and Zach had never been... it was lazy.

Heated skin pressed against her as Zach pressed himself against her bare breasts. The warmth of his skin set fire to nerve endings that should be drifting closer to sleep. As if he'd read her thoughts, Alex chuckled as he plastered himself against her back like a warm blanket.

"As much as my brother and I would love to answer that throaty moan, you need to rest."

Damn, damn, and double-damn. She hadn't even realized she moaned. Before she could respond, her legs folded out from under her. They caught her easily, but the damage was done. *Traitorous body!*

"Hold that thought, love. Zach will sleep with you for a couple of hours, then we'll see about sating your desire. I'll be in my office, wrapping up a few things for the club. Call me if she wakes up before I return."

Her last thought before falling into a blissful sleep was her regret Alex was leaving.

Chapter Sixteen

C ATALINA STEPPED CAREFULLY through the thick, dry undergrowth, scenting the unfamiliar flora, making certain nothing out of the ordinary lurked nearby. She'd been exploring ShadowDance Mountain, getting her bearings again after her strange experience yesterday. Something about her experience the day before felt too much like a warning for her peace of mind.

Today, she'd followed Brigitte's suggestion and focused on familiarizing herself with the perimeter, but the directions Alex Lamont gave her were sketchy at best. He'd been dead set against her going alone, only relenting when she'd explained she planned to shift before setting out. *Okay, saying he'd relented might be an exaggeration.*

The truth was she'd taken advantage of his silence when he'd only stopped objecting after being rendered speechless. It always amused her when the smartest people were the most surprised to learn the world around them wasn't as black and white as they imagined. Learning the full scope of magic and how it surrounded them always set people back on their heels.

Zach Lamont was less surprised since he'd seen her shift for himself, but he'd still seemed a bit surprised by the sheer scope of magical activity on ShadowDance Mountain. Since she didn't know much about either man, aside from what Ian McGregor had shared in casual conversation, Cat would reserve judgment about their acceptance.

The men had known shifters exist, but as Zach pointed out—hearing about something and getting to witness it for yourself are two completely different things. Being told was always more abstract and allowed for doubt. Seeing for himself left Zach without that small cushion of the uninformed. A woman's soft curse brought Catalina to a halt mid-step.

"Damn it all to the sun and moon. I know those clovers grow in this spot. I've seen them up here for years. Why the tarnation can't I find them today?" Peering through the thick branches of a young pine tree, Catalina was grateful she was in her wolf, keeping her from laughing out loud. The woman had to be pushing eighty, but the clothing she wore made her look like a hippy on steroids. Two different color high-top tennis shoes, wild colored striped socks, and frayed bellbottom jeans made Cat blink as she tried to reconcile the elderly woman and her outrageous clothing. Maybe the petite woman fried her brain with hallucinogens in the 60s. Cat knew Colorado had been a refuge for many of those who hadn't outgrown the counterculture movement of their youth.

According to the report she'd read on the flight from Texas, several of the small towns deep in the Rocky Mountains were originally founded by miners. Years later, the little hamlets were taken over by hippies who lived off the land, relishing the fact they needed little contact with the outside world. Now that she thought about it, Cat realized the woman in front of her might well be the oldest living hippy on earth.

"You might as well come out and say hello. I know you aren't from around here, or you'd already know I'm harmless. *Shazzle*, you might even be able to help me find the clovers. If I go back to the store without them, my damned sister is going to lecture me about wearing my specs. Goddess above, those things are a pain in my ass." Cat didn't know who she was, but she wasn't sure the spritely older woman needed her glasses if she'd spotted a wolf hidden twenty yards away.

Shifters had survived for thousands of years by avoiding humans they didn't know, particularly when they were in their wolf, so it took Cat a few seconds to convince herself it was safe to step out into the open. Taking a deep breath, Catalina ducked under the low branches and emerged into the small clearing. The woman stopped foraging to look at Catalina, studying her eyes without focusing on the rest of her wolf. Most humans were surprised by a shifter's size, and Cat couldn't remember the last time one of them looked into her eyes.

"There is something familiar about you. I don't know what just yet, but I will figure it out. Let me tell you, getting old isn't for sissies." She shook her head and chuckled, "I'd like to talk with you rather than to you." Digging into a satchel so large, Cat wondered how the diminutive woman carried the damned thing. The little spitfire muttered what sounded like an illumination spell before a bright light flared inside her cavernous bag.

With an exclamation of triumph, the petite bundle of energy pulled the ugliest coat Catalina had ever seen from the depths of the satchel and tossed it in front of Cat's wolf, then turned her back. Before she could think better of it, Cat shifted and pulled the coat around her.

"Thanks for the coat."

The woman turned around, the huge grin on her face until the light of recognition flared in her eyes.

"Brighten?" Shaking her head, the gesture making her wobble enough, Catalina moved quickly, reaching forward to steady her. "No, that can't be right. Brighten and her husband were killed in a car accident. Oh, my stars and garters... You're the Keeper of the Promises. You're the one the Magic Council has been watching. You're Catalina." *Keeper of the Promises?* The phrase sounded vaguely familiar, but Cat wasn't sure why.

"I'm afraid you have me at a disadvantage." The woman smiled at Catalina's polite reply before extending her hand.

"Opal Stone. I am thrilled to meet you. My sister and I own a magic shop near here. My sisters and I were friends with your great-grandmother, but that's neither here nor there and definitely a story for another day. What are you doing here?" When their hands first touched, Catalina felt the distinct sizzle of magical energy. She might not know who Opal Stone was in the great scheme of things, but there was no mistaking the intensity of the other woman's magical power.

"I'm sorry if I'm trespassing. I was worried I was no longer on ShadowDance Mountain, but Alex's directions were sketchy."

"Well, you are still on land owned by the Lamont family, but I'm afraid you're well beyond what locals consider

ShadowDance Mountain." The witch looked as though she was reading Catalina.

Her expression was one Cat had seen on Israel's face too many times to count. Taking time to look closely at Opal Stone, Catalina worked to hold back her smile. Opal's shoes were decorated with rhinestones and sequins, her striped knee-high socks were iridescent—evidently, she'd gotten the teen memo about life being too short to spend time matching socks—and the coat Opal wore dwarfed her, reminding Cat of the times she'd raided her brothers' closets.

"What did you mean when you called me the Keeper of the Promises?" Catalina saw the other woman stiffen before she'd even finished the question but assumed there was another issue when the witch seemed to be focusing her attention over Cat's left shoulder.

"Hello, Catalina. I see you've met my sister." Cat had only met Ola Stone a couple of times and hadn't made the connection between the two women. After all, Stone was a common name in the magical world. From what Cat remembered, Ola was a direct descendant of one of the oldest magical genetic lines.

"It's nice to see you again, Ola." Cat spun around and gasped. As a shifter, her enhanced hearing made it difficult for anyone to sneak up on her. She hated being startled and pressed her hand over her heart, trying to make certain it didn't beat out of her chest. Finding the ranking witch from the Magic Council standing within arm's reach was damned humbling.

Cat hated being dressed in nothing more than a borrowed coat. She was freezing now that she was back in her human form. Ola nodded once, and with a quick wave of her hand, Catalina found herself clad in jeans, boots, a wool sweater, and a thick down jacket. "Thanks. Did you just happen along, or were you looking for one of us?" Catalina didn't believe in coincidences.

"I was hoping to speak with you before anyone mentioned what many in the magical world consider your destiny." Ola's eyes briefly flickered to her sister, frustration pursing her brightly painted lips before her expression softened and her gaze returned to Cat. "You have the best of your mother's and father's skills. The Magic Council wants to speak with you about your future. We'd like to help you fulfill your destiny. Remember... great gifts come with greater responsibilities."

"I've just started a business I love. I have recently mated, and I can't imagine him being thrilled if I decided to live underground." Cat knew she was treading on thin ice, but the truth was, she didn't want to give up everything she'd work for all these years to become a trainee in some real-life version of Hogwarts.

"Cooper is already being actively recruited by the Council. We've been talking with him for some time. Your career plans and happiness are the reason our negotiations with Cooper have been stalled for so long. It's important you know there isn't a single council member who believes you should give up your career. Even though Ian McGregor isn't one of ours, the two of you are going to create a unique form of magic, working together. What we've seen in your future will keep a lot of people safe. You don't have to live underground. The apartment is for your convenience during meetings or training." Cat must have looked surprised when the other woman waved her hand, and a holographic image of a beautifully decorated apartment slowly rotated in front of her. When it disappeared, Ola chuckled. "It amuses me when magicals seem surprised to *see magic*—it defies logic."

"Don't be a snob, Ola. Catalina didn't have enough time with Brighten to be fully exposed to everything she should have learned. Why don't you be a mentor instead of a critic?"

"I'm not a snob. If you and Ruby are content up here in the middle of nowhere, selling trinkets and potions, it's none of my business."

Catalina might have been offended on Opal's behalf if she hadn't seen the twinkle in Ola's eyes. Cat and her sisters had similar long-standing battles that didn't mean anything, and she understood the underlying affection behind the banter. Listening to the two sisters bicker made her wish the five of them lived close enough to spend more time together.

"Such a tragedy... so many people killed by the dark forces trying to reassemble the magic totem. Your mother was a shining light among us, and even though all of the losses were felt deeply, hers was particularly painful." Catalina felt the burn of tears but refused to let them fall. Crying never changed anything. Opal's eyes seemed to glaze over for no more than a heartbeat before she grinned.

"There's a man closing in fast. I just got a glimpse of him in my mind's eye, but he's a looker." Opal looked over Cat's left shoulder, holding up five fingers, then four... three... two... one. Cat couldn't hold back her grin when Cooper burst through the thick brush.

"There you are. Holy shit, you move fast in your... Oh, I wondered who you were talking to." Smiling at Ola, he extended his hand. "Nice to see you again, Ola. Are you responsible for my mate's clothes? I was worried she was naked out here in the cold." His eyes flickered briefly to Opal, but it was easy to see he'd noticed the resemblance. Without waiting for an introduction, the flamboyantly dressed woman stepped forward to introduce herself.

"I was right—you're definitely a looker. Nice to meet you, young man. I'm Opal Stone. It seems you have already met my *older* sister." Catalina could have sworn she heard Ola growl, and it took every ounce of willpower she possessed to keep from smiling. Ola waved her hand in Opal's direction, but the sparks flying from the tips of her fingers bounced off what looked suspiciously like a clear shield. "Old tricks for old witches."

"You have always been a pain in my ass." Turning to Catalina and Cooper, Ola shrugged. "It's true. I am older... by ten minutes. You'd think it was ten years the way she carries on. And look at the way she dresses. I swear to the sweet Goddess, it's like she flunked out of Shriner Clown School."

"Ignore her, she's just jealous. Shopping at Fuddy-Duddies-R-Us sucks the happiness right out of people. I've seen it happen too many times to count... of course, they were all with Ola..."

Cat couldn't hold back her laughter any longer. She didn't care if the others were looking at her like she'd grown a second head. Within seconds, she could feel Cooper shaking with laughter from where he'd pressed against her back. When Catalina was finally able to take a breath, she swiped at the joyful tears rolling down her cheeks.

She hadn't laughed so hard since before her kidnapping. Something about the witches' banter opened the floodgates of her emotions—it felt as though all the fear and negativity of the past few months drained away. Was it their magic? Probably, but she didn't care. The only thing she could think about was how wonderful it felt to have her life back.

OLA STONE WATCHED Catalina closely, amazed at the change in her aura. The murky gray that had surrounded her for months evaporated into a mist as the younger woman's laughter filled the crisp mountain air. As twins, she and Opal had always been able to read each other in ways no one else ever fully understood. They'd sensed sadness lurking behind Catalina's calm exterior and had instinctively known what it would take to break through the veil the dark side tossed over her.

Ola doubted the young witch understood the curse she'd been living with or how much worse it would have been if Cooper hadn't gotten her out when he did. The men who'd been paid to detain her had gotten greedy and decided to extract information they could sell. Rather than notifying their bosses where they'd taken her, they'd tried playing both sides against the middle. Thank Goddess, Franklin Cordesi still had enough criminal and dark magic contacts to discover where she was being held. Cooper's rescue had come just in time. The physical injuries she'd sustained had been significant, but the dark magic she'd been repeatedly exposed to had been far worse. Franklin Cordesi's anonymous call to Cooper set up Catalina's rescue, but it had been Brigitte Stafford's alert last night that brought Ola to ShadowDance.

Ola had hoped to arrive before either of her sisters happened upon Catalina. But, as luck would have it, being the trouble magnet that she was, Opal had been front and center when Ola arrived. It had always amazed Ola how easily her sisters could find themselves in mischief. Ola knew Opal and Ruby would recognize Catalina on sight. The young witch's resemblance to her mother was uncanny. The dark magic masked some of the similarities, but the two of them had been friends with the family too long for Opal and Ruby to overlook. Some of her physical traits and the unique magical signature of Catalina's genetic line were unmistakable. Now, with the curse lifted, the resemblance was impossible to miss.

"Thank you. I haven't laughed so hard in so long, I was afraid I'd forgotten how. I've felt like I was living under a cloud since my rescue."

"Dark magic works in many ways, Catalina. Your mother didn't have time to teach you everything you need to know, or you would have recognized the spell you've been living under."

"Opal is right. By the time Brighten discovered they were being targeted because of the piece of the totem she was guarding, it was too late to teach you what you needed to know. She was supposed to leave you a letter instructing you to contact the council, but it seems to have slipped her mind." Ola knew Brighten wrote the letter—what she didn't know was what happened to it after her death.

"OH. WELL... SHOOT. I have the letter, but for so long, the pain was simply too raw to think about opening it. After my rescue, I knew I was teetering on the edge of imploding... I couldn't open it and risk losing my tenuous grip on sanity. I always felt it was slipping through my fingers." Cooper's arms came around her, cocooning her in his warmth and infusing her with his strength. She felt the hot burn of tears and knew she was going to lose the battle—damn, she hated crying. Some women looked like Southern belles when they cried. Catalina wasn't one of them.

"When you're ready. . we'll read it together, Princess. Remember, you don't have to face these things alone anymore."

His words were comforting, but Catalina knew it would take a while for her to fully embrace the fact she was mated. The relationship between fated mates was stronger than nonmagicals who were married. Divorce was unheard of—the bond between fated mates was so strong, most mates died within months of one another.

Are you reminding me to play it safe, so you don't follow me to the grave, mate?

Catalina was grateful Cooper's teasing pulled her back from an emotional ledge. Feeling a definite shift in the air around them, Catalina turned her focus to the two witches. Damn, for a couple of octogenarians, they moved much faster than Cat would have expected—before she could open her mouth to speak, they'd each taken a position on either side of where she and Cooper stood. Opal and Ola's backs were to the couple they were protecting, their bodies braced in the same defensive stance. Their wands magically appeared in their wrinkled hands—*not a good sign*. The most powerful witches rarely used their wands unless they were facing life-threatening danger.

The hair on the back of Catalina's neck stood on end as electricity crackled around them. Black smoke began to swirl several yards from where they stood, never fully taking shape. She caught glimpses of a human form, but the icy breeze made her eyes water too much to see clearly. Despite everything, the undeniable sense they were dealing with a powerful entity swept through her.

A feeling of sickening familiarity washed over her, and Catalina knew she'd encountered the same energy before. The moment she recognized it, Cat fought to stay in the moment. The last thing any of them needed was for her to tumble headlong into a flashback-fueled panic attack.

The mist swirled ominously closer but seemed to sense the threat posed by the Stone sisters. Trying to stay focused on the danger surrounding them wasn't easy when a flash of red lit up the area behind them. Within seconds, a third woman joined them. Dusting off her pants, she grinned before positioning herself with her back to Cooper's.

"Sorry, I'm late joining your little soiree. I was cleaning in the storeroom and didn't hear your message."

"Let me guess, you had your stereo blasting out oldies rock. You're going to ruin your hearing, Ruby." Opal's criticism must have rolled off her sister because all Cat heard from behind her was snickering.

"Don't get your bloomers in a twist. You know Steppenwolf's *Magic Carpet Ride* is meant to be played full-blast. It's not like you really need my help."

Holy Herman's Hermits, you called in the damned Calvary, and they are descending as we speak. Catalina was surprised when the woman's voice floated through her mind. *I'm Ruby Stone, the much younger sister, I'm sure these two have been raving about. Let me guess, Opal didn't find any of the clovers I need since she's about a thousand yards too far east. I swear she can't find her way out of a wet paper bag without GPS.*

Cooper's chest shook with laughter as he continued pressing against her back. Just what they needed, the damned dark magician to think they were laughing at him... or her. It seemed odd Catalina remembered not knowing the entity's gender during any of its visits while she'd been held in that damned squalid cell. The thought was followed by a more rapid swirling and tentacles reaching for her—the long fingers looking like something from the cartoons.

"Really? That's just lame. You didn't need to tell everybody I was in the wrong place. Damn, that's just mean. We called you so you wouldn't feel left out. Good grief, we know Mr. Smoke and Mirrors isn't a real threat." Opal's faux offended tone made Cat grin.

"Sister, don't challenge Little Donnie Dark. I bet he stayed up all night perfecting his scary look."

Oh, geez, now Ola's poking the bear.

"Don't you think it would be better if we waited until back-up arrives?" Cooper's question made Catalina rolled her eyes. Leave it to an operative to think... well, like an operative. He leaned over her shoulder, turning her face to his, a brow raised in challenge. "Did you just roll your eyes at me, Princess?" Oh, for the love of all things holy. He was going to go all Dom on her now? Did the man have no sense of self-preservation at all?

The dark swirl of energy drew nearer, nasty looking fingers moving closer and closer. The icy feel of the fingers stretching their reach toward her—the smoky tendrils were emitting a bone-chilling energy so terrifyingly familiar, it drove every rational thought from her mind.

I'm so glad you remember me, Catalina. Our time together in your rat-infested cell was cut short. Another day and you'd have come with me willingly.

Catalina's entire world narrowed to the voice echoing through her mind. When she tried to block it, pain lanced under her forehead. Wisps of memories she'd tried so hard to push out of her mind started to surface.

Aww, I see you are beginning to remember our conversations. Your mother was supposed to be mine. I'd spoken for her when she was still an infant in her mother's arms, but her family ignored my claim. I would have gained a gifted witch as my wife and access to the magnetic piece of the totem—the piece with the ability to pull the others to it. I didn't get the totem, but you'll make a fine wife. Together we'll swing magic's pendulum and rule over the dark side.

When no one else appeared to register the dark magician's menacing promise, Cat realized she was the only one who'd heard it. Knowing she'd been singled out sent ice racing through her veins.

You'll take her place. Your magic is more powerful than Brighten's. Purer in your innocence. If you had only stayed in that bloody cell just a little longer, you'd have been mine. I've waited, but now the time has come.

"No, I am already mated." She'd intentionally responded aloud to alert the others to what was happening. "I've
been claimed. You'll have to find another."

"No! You belong to me." This time the frightening
voice boomed all around them, the enraged sound filling
the entire area. Everyone around her jumped in surprise.
Before Catalina could open her mouth to respond, all hell
broke loose. Brilliant flashes of light, the clattering of what
sounded like swords, and an unearthly scream Cat knew
she'd hear in her nightmares forever. When the smoke
cleared, the three women surrounding them were covered
in dark smudges and what looked like thick oil.

"Fudge, I hate being slimed." Opal flicked her wrist,
sending a large glob of the foul-smelling goop sailing into
the air.

"That kids' television network thinks they dreamed up
sliming—what a joke. And lime green? It's just pathetic, I
tell you." Ruby moved to stand between her sisters,
looking from one to the other and giggling. "Guess I
shouldn't complain, you two look like you got the brunt of
it. What do you want to bet Audric looks like he just
stepped off the pages of GQ?"

"You flatter me, Ruby."

Catalina would have laughed if she hadn't been so
damned relieved to see the Magic Council's most powerful
wizard move out of the perimeter shadows. Ruby was
right—as usual, Audric Stafford looked like he'd just
stepped out of a men's fashion magazine, not a snow-white
hair out of place or a smudge anywhere to be seen. Brigitte
stomped out of the shadows, looking much worse for
wear.

"I don't know how he does it. I swear he is covered in the same non-stick coating as those frying pan hawkers sell on late-night television." With a simple wave of her hand, Brigitte fixed her clothing and everyone else's as well. "That shit has to go... it reeks of death and destruction... and I'm not in the mood."

"It happens when evil explodes." Audric gave them an apologetic smile before moving closer. Catalina laughed to herself at his pristine appearance. Her father had been the same way. He could walk through a burning coal mine and come out the other end with his white dress shirt crisp, clean, and looking as if he'd just picked up at the dry cleaners

"Too bad the bastard didn't evaporate sooner. I hate slime." Opal shook her head in disgust. Audric stopped in front of her and frowned as he took in her clothing.

"Goodness, who dressed you like an old lady?" Audric's tongue clicked, the scoffing sound so Old-World, Cat wanted to roll her eyes. "This will never do. No, indeed. It hurts my eyes to see you dressed in such depressing garb."

Catalina snickered as the conservative garments Brigitte had given Opal morphed into clothes Cat had only seen on American Bandstand and The Midnight Special. Good grief, she'd watched some old shows during her travels, and it showed.

Opal looked down at her new clothes and fist-pumped into the air. Bedazzled jeans, a shimmering silk shirt in the brightest shade of pink Cat had ever seen with a faux fur vest, topped pink sequined high-tops with rainbows on the side.

"Damn, skippy. These threads are cool. You always did

have excellent taste, Audric."

"Great Goddess, Audric, don't encourage her. At some point, she needs to start dressing like an adult." Ola rolled her eyes, but Catalina noted there wasn't any heat in her words.

Holding out his arms, Audric grinned when Ruby and Opal didn't hesitate to loop their wiry limbs with his. "Come on, ladies, let's go to the Lamonts. I happen to know they are expecting us. If we're lucky, they won't cover up that gorgeous glass table, and we'll get to enjoy some of their kinky foolery like that pretty girl said in that Fifty movie."

"Dad! Holy shit. Talk about too much damned information." Brigitte's full-body shudder made Cat grin. "We'll meet the four of you there." Without missing a beat, Brigitte grasped Catalina and Cooper by their upper arms, her grip surprisingly firm for such a petite woman. Before Cat could warn Cooper about what was coming, she heard the unmistakable whooshing of ley line travel. The last thing she heard before Cooper's gasp was Brigitte's muttered, "Hopefully, we'll get there in time to warn the Lamonts about the geriatric hippy invasion."

Chapter Seventeen

C OOPER HAD NEVER experienced motion sickness until now—and it sucked. "Fuck me. You could have warned me. What the hell was that about? Shit, I need to sit down." Looking around, he was relieved to see they were on the Lamonts' patio. Damn, some efficient do-gooder had already put the outdoor furniture close to the building in preparation for winter storage. When a chair materialized out of thin air behind him, Cooper dropped into it and hoped his stomach would settle when his head finally stopped spinning.

"Ley line." Brigitte's reply was followed by a disinter-ested wave of her hand, indicating she considered the two words the only explanation required. Cooper had astral traveled before, but that slow slide was nothing compared to what he'd just experienced. He also knew Cleveland Adler and his wife Vienna utilized ley lines when astral traveling, but no one mentioned how disorienting the process was. Jesus, Joseph, and Sweet Mother Mary, was this mode of travel this nauseating for everybody? Did magicals ever get accustomed to it, or did Brigitte pull something special out of her little bag of tricks just to make his life more challenging? Slapping his palm against his forehead at the stupid question, he wondered how much longer he'd feel like he'd spent the last twenty-four hours strapped into some damned amusement park torture device.

"It'll get better, Ace. I'm surprised it bothered you since you've survived my driving on several occasions. Of course, there have been a few incidents when you looked a little worse for wear." Catalina's driving was the one area of her life where his remarkable mate was utterly out of control.

"What saves me with your driving is gravity. This,"— he made a swirling motion with his index finger—"was ass-over-teakettle, as my mother used to say. Something akin to being caught in a vertical tornado with a flash of brilliant colors." He wasn't sure he'd be able to find the words to describe the experience to someone who hadn't been subject to it. It was one of those things you had to experience firsthand to understand.

"It isn't my preferred way to travel, either, but it's fast and free. Not all ley lines are created equal, and the one running beneath us is powerful." Gigi gave a disinterested shrug before adding, "It's probably too powerful for such a short trip." Sucking in a deep breath, Cooper felt his body respond to his silent, internal command to calm down.

"Short trips are intense because you have the disorientation of liftoff and landing—for lack of better words— without getting to experience the beauty usually present in between." Catalina knelt beside him, her warmth seeping in to calm him in a way nothing else could. Within a few seconds, he felt normal once again and breathed in a sigh of relief he hadn't embarrassed himself by vomiting all over the flagstone patio.

"Wow, that was a really scary shade of green, Cooper." Looking up, Cooper met Katarina Lamont's dancing blue eyes and smiled. "I wasn't trying to eavesdrop. I saw a strange flash of light out here and came to investigate. You looked pretty peaked, so I didn't want to move around a lot or startle you by speaking."

"Thanks. It was touch and go for a few minutes. I've never been motion sick—I don't recommend it."

A wicked grin spread over Katarina's face, but her eyes still shone with kindness. "People who get motion sick easily don't usually like Colorado. Our mountain roads aren't for the faint of heart. Just driving through on Interstate 70 makes a lot of people queasy." Katarina shrugged. "I've never been motion sick, but I've heard it feels like morning sickness, and that sucked big green donkey dicks."

"Kitten, I don't know what we're going to do with you. I thought we'd erased that expression from your vocabulary."

"I'm living proof the First Amendment is alive and well." The irrepressible woman gave a parade wave to the invisible masses before turning on her heel to return to the house. "Come inside, it's getting chilly, and I'm sure I heard the doorbell."

Walking alongside Zach, Cooper shook his head. "Let's go talk to Alex—you're not going to believe what I just saw." Two years ago, there were only a handful of people Cooper trusted. A late-night conversation with his sister changed everything.

Yes, opening yourself up means you might get hurt, but

watching you exist rather than live is breaking my heart. You deserve so much more, Cooper.

Now, his circle of trusted friends was exponentially larger, and his life felt full for the first time in years. After his parents died, his world had narrowed, his boundaries drawing closer and closer until he could practically touch the walls he'd built around himself. Lakyn had loved him unconditionally, and he was always humbled by how resilient she remained when he'd turned colder and more distant. Now, he could see the only other woman he'd ever loved to the depths of his soul shared his sister's warrior spirit.

Catalina Adler was the most courageous woman he'd ever known. She'd risked her life for her country more times than he could count and put her own dreams on the back burner to help ensure the safety of agents from intelligence agencies all over the world. Their agencies might have turned their backs on Catalina in her time of need, but Cooper knew their agents were loyal as hell to her. Maybe he'd invite some of them to the open house she'd been forced to push back time and again.

Stepping into Alex's office, Cooper was surprised to see Franklin Cordesi sitting in one of the leather wingback chairs chatting with Audric. Shaking Cordesi's hand, Cooper wondered if the man was ever going to own up to making the anonymous call giving him the location where Catalina had been held. His call saved her life, and Cooper wanted to thank him properly, but Franklin's coy smile let him know that was going to be a conversation for another day.

Two hours later, Alex and Zach both appeared shell-shocked. They looked stunned to learn about the magical battle that had taken place on their property. Katarina's eyes sparkled with interest, her expression reminding him of his sister when she'd been younger, and everything had seemed to catch her interest. After a tension-filled silence in their long conversation, Alex leaned back and sighed before turning his attention to Catalina.

"You've been an interesting guest, Catalina. My one regret is my dad wasn't here. His ancestors have passed down stories for many years about the epic battles good and evil waged on these mountains. He told me once, you could feel the pulse of the earth beneath your bare feet if you could still your mind long enough to connect with something bigger than yourself."

"I'd love to meet your father." Audric leaned forward, his eyes twinkling with interest.

"I've always been fascinated by Native American folk-lore. Your father is right. The ley line running through this area is one of the most powerful on earth. Ironically, your home, the meadow we were in, and the Stone sisters' store in Crystal, are all in perfect alignment atop the ley line." No one spoke for long seconds as Audric gave the group time to absorb what he'd said.

"Great Goddess, Dad, cut the dramatic pauses. Get on with it. I'm starving." Gigi glanced toward the door they all knew led to the kitchen. When Catalina's stomach growled loud enough for the entire room to hear, Audric laughed out loud.

"I'm more relieved than I can tell you, Catalina is safe. The Council has agreed to work with her part-time until she is ready for something more intense." Turning to Opal and Ruby, Audric grinned. "Don't worry too much about Emerald. I believe your granddaughter is going to make some big changes in her life very soon. Ironically, the line we're sitting on runs within a few yards of her house."

"When can I go home?" Catalina's question surprised everyone but Cooper—he'd felt the undercurrent rolling through her and knew she was anxious to get back to work. The renovations had been completed on their home in the Adler Oil building and everyone was withholding pictures because they wanted to see her reaction firsthand. "Sorry, I don't mean to sound ungrateful, and I'll never be able to repay you for your hospitality, but I waited years to start my business, and leaving in the hands of other people wasn't easy."

"I've packed your bags, and there is a plane waiting to take you back to Texas in an hour." Gigi grinned before casting a longing look toward the kitchen.

"We'll eat first. I know Audric is looking forward to seeing your table." Catalina laughed when the elderly wizard's cheeks turned pink.

"I always knew you'd be trouble."

Epilogue

"**I** CAN'T BELIEVE you're seriously thinking about moving to Colorado." Paris Adler blew over the top of her steaming mug of hot chocolate and frowned at her friend. "If you know your grandmother and great-aunt are blowing smoke up your ass, why go?"

"You're whining, Paris." London's comment earned her a narrow-eyed glare, but she appeared unphased by her youngest sister's hostility.

"I'm not whining. I am simply trying to get Emerald to see abandoning her independence would be a Goliath-sized mistake."

"You mean abandoning *you*." London's unwelcome interjection earned her a scathing muttered curse about a woman who needs two men to keep her in line, making Emerald Stone lean her head back bursting into a gale of laughter.

"I haven't decided to move. At this point, it's just something Granny Good Witch is trying to sell… okay, *sell* might be a bit of an understatement, but you get the idea. She really stepped up her effort after meeting Catalina. It seems she appreciated the energy generated by being near a *youngster*—that's a direct quote, by the way."

"Eli said there is a really great kink club not far from where your family lives—which probably explains why Cam stashed Cat and Cooper there until the threat to her was neutralized. The ShadowDance Club is owned by Alex and Zach Lamont. Evidently, the Lamonts are long-time friends of Ian's." London waggled her arched eyebrows at Emerald, whose cheeks immediately turned scarlet.

"It's a given the club is great if they are friends of Ian's. I know there is a network of clubs that all adhere to the same safe, sane, and consensual standards. If there is a problem with a member or visitor in one club, the information is shared with the others." London smiled smugly when Paris stared at her in surprise.

London might have two mates, but she was notoriously private, even with those in the lifestyle. Hearing her talk about kink clubs in front of Emerald was unexpected... and suspicious—very suspicious indeed.

"Did I tell you Audric Stafford is stopping by to see me tomorrow? When I asked if my family was okay, he laughed and assured me they are fine. I'm not really a part of the magic world, so it seems odd he's coming to visit, don't you think?" Paris and London looked at each other and sighed.

"Have a safe trip to Colorado, Em."

The End

Books by Avery Gale

The Adlers
Brooklyn
London
Austin
Paris
Cleveland
Asia
Kensington
Israel
Bronx
Catalina

The ShadowDance Club
Katarina's Return – Book One
Jenna's Submission – Book Two
Rissa's Recovery – Book Three
Trace & Tori – Book Four
Reborn as Bree – Book Five
Red Clouds Dancing – Book Six
Perfect Picture – Book Seven

Club Isola
Capturing Callie – Book One
Healing Holly – Book Two
Claiming Abby – Book Three

Masters of the Prairie Winds Club
Out of the Storm
Saving Grace
Jen's Journey
Bound Treasure
Punishing for Pleasure
Accidental Trifecta
Missionary Position
Another Second Chance
Star-Crossed Miracles
Dusted Star
Lilly's Choice

The Wolf Pack Series
Mated – Book One
Fated Magic – Book Two
Tempted by Darkness – Book Three

The Knights of the Boardroom
Book One
Book Two
Book Three

The Morgan Brothers of Montana
Coral Hearts – Book One
Dancing with Deception – Book Two
Caged Songbird – Book Three
Game On – Book Four
Well Bred – Book Five

Mountain Mastery
Well Written

Savannah's Sentinel
Sheltering Reagan

The Christmas Painting
Taking Out the Mother of the Bride

I would love to hear from you!

Email:
avery.gale@ymail.com

Website:
www.averygale.com

Facebook:
facebook.com/avery.gale.3

Twitter:
@avery_gale